The Gardener Through History

Robin Johnson

Publisher: Inspiring Publishers,
P.O. Box 159, Calwell, ACT Australia 2905
Email: publishaspg@gmail.com
http://www.inspiringpublishers.com

A catalogue record for this book is available from the National Library of Australia

National Library of Australia The Prepublication Data Service

Author: Robin Johnson
Title: The Gardener Through History
Genre: Non-fiction
ISBN: 978-1-922792-19-8

Contents

Foreword

How far back in history does humanity have to go when exploring the development of modern day food we see on our supermarket shelves.

At the outset, of my book I would like to recognise the contribution of James H.S. McGregor's book, *Back to the Garden*, in providing me inspiration and a sound basis for the composition of my book. He suggests that 'First Nature' is the basis of all environmental considerations.

McGregor provides insights and thoughts of early humanity on the edges of the Mediterranean (Mesopotamia). The first domesticated plants were farmed around the edges of the Mediterranean where wheat, barley, lentils and types of peas were grown. People in other parts of the world - including eastern Asia, parts of Africa and parts of North and South America - also domesticated plants.

Finding an appropriate starting point for my book was a significant undertaking. Research took me back to the Neanderthal tribesmen, who lived through the harsh cold climates of Britain and Europe and tamed the natural landscapes. They began growing fundamental food crops that McGregor refers to as 'First Nature' and were the instigators of the first agricultural revolution that changed the world forever. Then the story moves to Britain's Middle Ages which witnessed the beginning of sustainable agriculture.

The beginning of agriculture across the Cyprus, in the Mediterranean and southern France can be traced to the discovery of cave paintings and fossil records. These discoveries in southern

France reinforced the impact of the Neanderthal tribesmen on the first agricultural revolution. They foraged for food by wandering by foot for many miles through the plains of Europe. Some 10,000 years ago, they domesticated wild plants between the Tigris and Euphrates rivers (the embryo of life) by collecting the seeds of cereal grains to resow and grow. This enabled them to settle down and form small communities. These basic food crops, which were part of the diet of Neolithic people, continue to feed the world today.

During the Neanderthal period, the country around the Mediterranean and throughout Europe and Britain was heavily forested, with large roaming mammals (now extinct). In 1995, a cave was discovered in southern France (the Chauvet Cave) with paintings of animals roaming through the countryside and illustrations of how the Neanderthals sustained themselves. They used a red ochre pigment to paint images of wild horses, lions, bison, mammoths and rhinoceroses on the walls of the caves. It is now a cave of world significance and gives us an insight into the realities of life during the Neolithic period.

The food of the Neanderthals fell into three types: the legumes which are high in lysine, peas, beans and an early lentil; tuber, potato, sweet potato and parsnip (the swollen root); and an early leaf vegetable called vetch, which was a bitter lettuce. The cereals wheat and barley have been known since the Iron Age - they depleted the soil's nutrients, whereas the legumes replenished the soils.

The first agricultural revolution is indebted to this historical period, when early humans domesticated and cultivated these cereal crops. It was this period that was responsible for much of the cereal and organic food we eat today.

People first domesticated plants about 10,000 years ago (written in ancient Scripture) between the Tigris and Euphrates rivers (the embryo of life) in Mesopotamia (which includes the modern countries of Iran, Iraq, Turkey and Syria). Early people collected and planted the seeds of wild plants. To begin the process of domestication, early humans made sure that plants had water, and planted them in areas to receive sunshine. Seeds germinated weeks or months later, and plants blossomed, and food crops were harvested.

My book explains in plain English how the world's agricultural history originated with the Iron Age in Britain and progressed through each historical period, including the Middle Ages where I discuss the pros and cons of the three-field system. In our modern world, we take for granted that sowing seed will give us domesticated plants. However, plants were first raised from the wild and cared for by humans. Domesticated species are not wild.

Finally I would like to include an edited version of an article that grew out of a presentation given by M.Z. Zedar at the Calpe 2007 Symposium: People in the Mediterranean–A History of Interaction, September 27–30, 2007, the Gibraltar Museum, Gibraltar.

MZ Zedar suggested that the recognition of the broader role of humans in shaping post-Neolithic environments is central to understanding how Mediterranean biodiversity evolved and how we might best work to conserve it. The archaeological sciences have a valuable role to play in providing greater time depth to biodiversity studies by monitoring the creation of anthropogenic ecosystems and tracing the development and impacts of both environmentally sustainable and destructive agricultural economies over thousands of years of human occupation.

I then explore organic food production with gardening concepts of the 18ᵗʰ and 19ᵗʰ century, before finally discussing World War 2 vegetable growing with the allotment system. I conclude by considering the sustainable garden for our modern world.

Why am I writing this book?

"I have always been captivated by the origin of growing organic food, also with a keen interest in history, I decided that growing organic food has to have its own history."

Introduction

I spent my childhood and young adult life in England, where my family and I would walk the country lanes searching the hedgerows for edible fruit, roots and leaves. We found a variety of wild berries amongst the village hedgerows, including blackberry, raspberry, blueberry and sloe. We would also dig wild roots that included small turnips, parsnips and picked vetch (wild lettuce). These experiences were the foundation for my ongoing passion for gardening.

While growing up in Britain and subsequently spending time in the United States, I also developed a keen interest in social history, especially during my horticultural and gardening career. In addition, I have enjoyed visiting some outstanding public gardens such as Blenheim Palace and Hidcote Gardens in Britain, and Mount Vernon in Virginia in the United States. I have always wanted to talk to the gardeners of these three spectacular examples of well-developed and elaborate gardens.

In 1984, after arriving in Australia, I won a position as a gardener-in-charge of the grounds of the Old Parliament House in Canberra. I was one of the seven full-time gardeners who looked after the old rose gardens within the confines of the Cupressus hedges, and was also responsible for the flowering annuals planted each year. I learnt quicky that it was the 'attention to detail work' that was paramount to ensure all practical gardening functions were fulfilled to the highest quality of expertise.

As gardeners, we were responsible for pruning roses, planting annual displays, lawn care maintenance, mowing and top dressing the lawns. Working at the Old Parliament House reinforced my historical interest in gardening and the political systems we have developed through history.

Years later, when I began to consider writing my third book (the first being *Garden Design for Everyone*, and the second *Your Sustainable Garden*), I mulled over the popularity today of eating organic food. I wanted to know the history of organic growing. In our modern world, shoppers are presented with the label 'organically grown' in retail fruit and vegetable shops. However, I wanted to write the story from a gardener's perspective - this idea finally brought growing and social history together.

As I began researching this topic, I became interested in Neolithic Britain, or the Stone Age. These early Britons scavenged for edible plants growing in Britain's earliest natural surroundings (native landscape before any human interaction).

Chapter 1 begins by describing early gardening practices in the Neolithic era. While researching, I realised how important this era was to our modern-day society. These early Britons pictured the universe as a partnership between themselves, the land and the communities around them They collected wild cereal seed which, over hundreds of years of cultivation, has changed some of its genetic composition.

In Chapter 2, I explore Britain's Roman occupation (43 AD to 410 AD). The Romans were excellent gardeners and being an occupational force, they soon settled into Britain's way of life. I describe the interaction of Roman gardeners with early Britons and how they grew a wide range of vegetables and introduced 'Madder'.

In Chapter 3, I scrutinise the farmers of the early Middle Ages and their methods of growing crops in the three-field system. This was the true beginning of organic farming. I focus on the small-scale peasant gardeners and discuss the impact of significant climate change (an increase in sunspot activity and the advent of the Little Ice Age) that affected the northern hemisphere and resulted in horrendous social and economic upheaval.

My attention then moves to the monasteries of the 10th-12th centuries - the Monks were highly educated, skilled and organised gardeners. They created magnificent kitchen gardens inside and outside their monasteries, growing early lettuce, onions, carrot, radish, dill, coriander, chervil and parsley. They also grew flowers such as the marigold, cornflowers and daisies. The gardeners of the monasteries became well respected members of society.

In Chapter 4, I reflect on the great social upheaval of the 1500s and the significant social and economic change that occurred throughout Europe between 1500 and 1850, including the Industrial Revolution which saw many farm inventions come to the fore. This was the time of the herbalists, the first growers to appreciate the medicinal value of many herbal plants. Courtesy of the ocean explorers, many new vegetables began to arrive from the Americas such as tomatoes and potatoes which were looked upon as a novelty. Cauliflowers and orange carrots (carrots were previously white or purple) were introduced and first grown in Britain during the late 1590s. The artichoke was a prize to be grown, often commanding its own special enclosed garden.

In Chapter 5, my focus turns to the early garden writers who wrote some of the first horticultural books during the 1500s and early 1600s. This period was characterised by the beginning of printing and the emergence of early garden writers. I first write about Simon Harward (1572-1614) who wrote a book titled *A New Orchard and Garden*. I then briefly consider Marcus Woodward and L.H. Bailey who wrote a book in 1923 titled

Manual of Gardening: A Practical Guide to the Making of Home Grounds and the Growing of Flowers, Fruits, and Vegetables for Home Use.

(For this piece, I was lucky to be able to tap into an extremely rare reference book titled *Leaves from Gerards Herball* with arrangements by Marcus Woodword. This book was first published in 1597, then enlarged and amended by Thomas Johnson in 1633. The first modern version was edited by Marcus Woodward in 1927).

Chapter 6 is set in the 20th Century when the relative calm of Europe was displaced by two World Wars. During the early part of the 20th Century, the 'victory garden' became a catch cry of the vegetable growers. I also cover the period of strong growth and prosperity that followed World War II.

I examine gardeners who worked on their vegetable allotments and suburban gardens. The earliest lawn mowers were horse-drawn, but eventually became more sophisticated and common around large homes. From the 1960s onwards, the cities became increasingly busy, and private home owners resorted to employing gardeners and lawn mower men. The sounds of contractors mowing lawns became a familiar sound of summer across many of the suburbs from the 1970s onwards.

Looking forward, what does the future have in store for the gardener and the garden in a world affected by climate change? Chapter 7 suggests that society will have to consider how it values suburban gardens in the future. I note how private gardens and commercial agricultural enterprises will experience significant fluctuations in rainfall patterns, followed by long droughts. I discuss the need for water storage and how it will become an essential component of gardens and large agricultural properties.

Throughout the book, I have endeavoured to focus on the gardeners' knowledge and the value of their labour. Through each historical period, it is important for society to determine what value it places on the work of its gardeners. It is interesting to note that despite many technological advances over time, the gardener's tools of trade have not changed markedly – the spade, fork, rake and hoe are still used by modern day gardeners as much as they were hundreds of years ago.

In his book,[1] *Back to the Garden* (2015), James H S McGregor debates the process he calls 'first nature', as distinct from the more familiar term 'second nature'. He suggests that 'first nature' is the basis of all environmental considerations.

An interpretation of first and second nature is as follows:

First Nature:[2] This is an instinctive/basic function in nature – for example, the earth's seasons of Spring/Summer/Autumn/ Winter are uniquely different to each other and follow one another in perfect order to sustain life due to the earth's angle in relation to the sun. This is a naturally occurring phenomenon.

Another example of [2] first nature is the germination of wild ripe seeds at different rates depending on the thickness of their husks - some seeds spend years in the ground before germinating. On the other hand, seed that is domesticated loses most of its protein level and is replaced with starch. Wild seed is rich in protein, whereas domesticated seed is richer in fatty acids and starch.

Second Nature: This is the acquisition of subject knowledge (e.g., seed sowing) and being able to perform the skill naturally (all modern humans have a skill that comes as second nature).

---

1 *Back to the Garden* (2015), James H S McGregor
2 ibid

Welcome to my book, *The Gardener Through History*. I hope it takes you on a fascinating journey from Neolithic Britain to the Middle Ages and through to modern times, as it explores the role and value of gardeners during each historic period.

Prologue

Combustion and fire

From the research I have undertaken for this book, 'fire' has been the main force for sustaining life on Earth. While no one can provide absolute timing for the discovery and first use of fire by early Neolithic tribesmen, there is no doubt that the Earth at that time was ablaze with volcanic and earthquake eruptions that have helped shape our modern landscape.

I begin writing *The Gardener Through History* by explaining that Neolithic hunters and gathers eventually settled down to create domesticated village life. The collection, storage and resowing of wild cereal seed began the process of its domestication. These practices then morphed into the Neolithic Revolution and the use of fire. Historians have long considered these acts as prime evidence of the development of human intelligence. Indeed, Neolithic tribesmen found that their use and control of fire distinguished them from other primitive humans that roamed Europe and Britain during this period.

To think of fire, one must firstly consider what Earth was like before humans appeared. While it was undoubtedly a burning mass, it is clear that for fire to sustain itself it firstly needs fuel to burn; and secondly, it needs oxygen. Thirdly, there must be a heat or ignition source that allows a fire to begin. These elements must have been available on Earth. We wouldn't expect fire to burn on a barren Earth, so there would have been plant life to provide a fuel source.

As indicated by Time Magazine in 2018, vegetation fires can't occur until the oxygen level in the atmosphere has reached around 15% (it is 21% today). This is why we smother a fire with a blanket or sand, pump carbon dioxide on it, or even flood it with water to extinguish it[3].

Modern evidence of fire in fossil records is reliant on charcoal that stays in the soil. Charcoal is the partially burnt plant material left after a fire has been through an area. The oldest fire recorded on Earth has been identified from charcoal in rocks formed during the late Silurian Period, around 420 million years ago[4].

Historically, plants spread throughout the Earth during this period. However, my research suggests that there seemed to be fluctuating levels of oxygen. The first recorded extensive wildfires occurred later, around 350 million years ago during the early Carboniferous period.

To begin my journey of gardening, I investigate the Earth's early history when oxygen levels in the atmosphere were higher than they are today for extensive periods. During these times, fires would have been hotter and more frequent. I understand that one of the high-fire intervals in the Earth's history occurred during the later stages of the Cretaceous period, when dinosaurs ruled the Earth and flowering plants first appeared.

It is interesting to note that in Australia many plants have adapted well to a fiery landscape. A selection of pines, eucalypts and proteas were among the first that appeared around some 90 million years ago and actually need fire to reproduce. Neolithic tribesmen learnt to use fire to burn nature to create pasture and fields to grow early wheat, and to eventually create gardens close to early villages.

---

3 Andrew C Scott, *When Did Humans Discover Fire?* Time Magazine, June 2018
4 Ibid

They learnt to manage First Nature wild landscapes all across Europe and Britain. Fire also spread throughout the grasslands and savannas of Africa around 7 million years ago. Fire has made a big impact, not only on the plant environment but also on the animal kingdom.

It is important to understand the effect of fire on early humans. In his book, *Fire*, Stephen J. Pyne[5] explores fire's long advancement with humanity. He examines fire's influence on landscapes, art and science, and its relationship with climate change in more recent times. The hottest summers, together with the worst bushfires in history, have been attributed to significant changes in climate.

5 Stephen J Pyne, *Fire – a Second Edition*, NewSouth Publishing, 2020

Chapter 1

The Gardener
Through History

Neolithic Britain: (Britain's New Stone Age).10,000BC-2000BC, lasting for approximately 2.5 million years

To begin the gardener through history we need to ask ourselves *'where did the first farmers come from?' I have included a part of a summary written by* [1] *Josh Davis 2019"The introduction of farming during the Neolithic era changed the course of human history. In Britain, the island's entire culture changed, incorporating new making pottery, tools and obituary practices"*.

To begin this history of gardening, it is also important to have an appreciation of the climatic environment during Britain's prehistory – that is, the period before human events were recorded in writing.

During that period, the climate transitioned from a considerably cold period to an extensive warm period. The warming of the earth was fundamental to the creation of an environment conducive to the cultivation of crops and plants.

A study of Britain's early tribes during the Neolithic period (Bronze and Iron Age) – reveals that they began as traditional hunters and gatherers, and slowly began to settle into villages and larger communities, tilling the land over time to become farmers with a good understanding of growing seed crops in settlement enclosures. As their population expanded, they slowly removed much of Britain's natural forest cover.

These communities kept small, protected gardening plots close to their villages and inside their communities. These plots were hedged predominately with an early hawthorn plant, established by striking winter cuttings. Protected from wild animals, the plots eventually gave rise to an early broad bean, early beets, tall celery like vegetables, early peas and onion tubers.

But Josh Davis [2] goes on to ask "*where did farming and tilling the land to grow cops come from? And what happened to the hunter-gatherers already living in Britain?* Genome sequencing at the Museum of Natural history in London has been providing the modern world with answers.

Through this sequencing farming culture arrived in Britain about 6,000 years ago, marking the beginning of the Neolithic period in Britain. (New Stone Age)[1].

Previously, in the Mesolithic period (Middle Stone Age) Britain had been home to a population of hunter-fisher-gatherers.

This transition to farming marked a huge shift to organised life in Britain. It is still debated whether the arrival of Neolithic farming cultures represented Britain's early population adopting new practices or was it the arrival of migrant farmers coming over from continental Europe.

The first agricultural revolution

During Britain's Stone Age, early humans foraged an existence by hunting, gathering and fighting with other tribes to maintain their use of the land around their settlements.

Britain's Bronze Age (Metal Age): 2,500 BC – 500 BC

The Bronze Age began when tin was discovered in Cornwall, South West England, around 1600 BC by invaders from the continent who swept through Cornwall and the south west of Britain. They settled in the south west to help the locals find large tin deposits in the area. They learnt how to produce bronze by smelting and mixing copper with tin.

The coming of the Bronze Age was a giant leap forward in the journey of humanity. Bronze was found to be much harder and more durable than other metals available at the time, allowing Bronze Age civilizations to gain a technological advantage. This knowledge was passed on to the Romans when the farming communities learnt to make the metal plough.

The settlers of south west Britain tilled the soil and began to grow crops on the land. They fought other tribes for control of the forests and streams, and created gardens and grew crops. They learnt to domesticate wild animals by building fences to form enclosures. They raised chickens, cattle and oxen to provide meat and milk for nourishment, and used their hides for warmth. This was the beginning of crop growing and agriculture.

These early farmers learnt to save seed and store it for planting the following year. Unfortunately, the population during this period was illiterate and, to this day, we have only a few stone monuments (stone circles, Stonehenge) as a record of activities.

The Celtic Tribe Era: Approximately 700 BC

Around 700 BC, there seemed to be a massive movement of tribes of Celtic origin spreading west across Europe, predominantly from around the Danube and central Europe. The tribes had a great understanding of agriculture, growing and storing grains, tending livestock and using primitive farm implements. The Celtic tribesmen were blonde haired and had a love for bright colours and making fine jewellery. Their tribes were very organised, settling and joining with Britain's native tribes. Their ranks descended from the priestly Druids to the slave who worked the land.

The Celtic tribes bought to Britain great farming skills and were renowned for producing two crops a year in Britain's climate. Wild pears, strawberries, sloe, nuts, Fat Hen (with its rich seeds,) celery, leafy brassicas and carrots were all crops grown by Celtic farmers.

Note: The Iron Age Hill Fort Sidbury Hill Hampshire UK is an example of an iron age hill fort built in approximately 500 BC

It is located in Hampshire, England, north-west of Winchester. It is more than just 'a hill fort': since the Celtic era, archaeologists have ensured that it has become one of the most intensely studied hill forts in Britain. It still exhibits a round dwelling with grain storage pits surrounded by mighty earthen walls. The site covers approximately 12 acres and was purchased by Hampshire County Council in 1958

The Iron Age Hill Fort, Sidbury Hill Hampshire

Britain's Iron Age:-Bronze Age 800 BC - AD 43

The Iron Age was characterised by significant technological and social advances. Metal tools were made to use on the land and pottery of fine quality was also produced. This period represented a significant step forward in agriculture, with the use of metal farm implements, right up to the beginning of Britain's Roman occupation.

At this stage in history, Britain was an agricultural community, with its inhabitants living and tilling the land, and growing crops such as early wheats, spelt and maize. People settled into villages and fenced compounds. They were skilful, having learnt to use fire to produce metalwork, including weaponry.

An archaeological site in Cambridgeshire, known as Flag Fen, has revealed the remains of a huge complex of Bronze Age and Iron Age remains. Some settlements in this area have lasted for more than 2000 years.

I stated earlier that tribes living in the Neolithic period had little or no writing skills. Our knowledge of these early humans is provided by archaeology, such as stone henge and other stone monuments scattered throughout Britain; along with a few Greek and Latin texts, all which proved to be an important turning point in our understanding of this prehistoric era.

They struggled through some of the harshest and coldest weather of all time with giant icebergs floating down through the North Sea from Iceland, coming as far south as the Scottish border. Britain and Europe was a greatly different place than it is today, with vast areas of wilderness, with roaming tribes fighting for their share of Britain's or Europe's natural resources.

Early tribes hunted through Britain's natural landscape for food, eventually settling, into communities, beginning to till the soil, with an early plough, and grow seed they had collected.

The Neolithic Revolution:

As well as several species of early wheat, they found growing wild and grew on early farms an early cabbage, broccoli, a 'root like' carrot, parsnip and red beet, which now forms the basis of food for all humans.[1] Simply by sowing and harvesting seed from early grasses they had collected, the Neolithic people without realising changed the complete make- up of the wild seed.

Over time this wild seed genes became domesticated producing a whole new generic species, a domesticated seed that produced a thinner husk, compared to the wild one which was a seed with a thicker husk.

The Neolithic tribesmen foraged and collected berries and domesticated the wild cereal seed (thick husk grasses) such as (elkhorn wheat, emmer wheat and barley.

Barley (Hordeum vulgare) became domesticated, as its spikes became 'non shattering' that made it easier to harvest on maturity.

Barley continues to be a major cereal grain grown globally in temperate climates. It is important to consider that in the wild, all thick husk cereal grasses (barley, oats, wheat) germinated at different times and rates depending on their fall to the ground and thickness of their husk, some staying dormant for two seasons, only germinating when conditions are right, germinating slower they can survive hot and dry summers before sprouting.

Whereas thin husked domesticated cereal seed germinates quicker however full of starch, and lower in proteins and oils, they also have a drop in nutrients protein starches, and fatty acids.

Grasses, that rapidly shed their seed (those with a thin husk) on maturity were inclined not to be gathered the following year by early farmers, meaning they were not stored and planted the following season.

Those with small seeds or bitter taste were also seen as undesirable. The rhythm of continual sowing and reaping of these vital grasses (Barley, Wheat, Oats), favours the thinner husks, but have less nutritional value than its wild counterpart, all now form the basis of the cereals that continue to feed the planet and stock our supermarket shelves today. The Neolithic tribesman also found four wild legumes (lentil, pea, bitter vetch and chickpea). They banded together to capture prehistoric animals of the time such as mammoth, early tigers and deer pigs, goats, sheep, and cattle. Over this extensive time period the domestication of seed Neolithic tribesmen settled into hamlets and became the first farmers by learning how to use oxen and a primitive plough to till the land.

The Neolithic tribesman also caught fish in Britain's rivers, ate wild herbs, early roots such as carrots, and parsnips dock leaves, nettles an early lentil and chickpea. They also found fruits such as wild apples. These became one of of the first crops to be grown in enclosures that surrounded their villages. Raspberries and blackberry, and nuts including the hazelnut, were also found at this time. An early flax was used for weaving a thatch for the village huts.

Note 1: The Neolithic tribesmen became extinct with their adaptation into the modern human being. Together great climatic change of the earth, and a period serious diseases. The Neolithic tribesmen over thousands of years replaced by early modern humans some 800,000 years later

Note 2: The term 'Neolithic Revolution' was coined by V. Gordon Childe [3] in his 1936 book Man Makes Himself.

Iron age-Roman gardening in Britain, dates :880BC-43AD

The Ancient Grains through an Historical Time line

1. Spelt (Triticum Spelta)

Spelt went by the name of 'Farro Grande' and was originally cultivated in Iran and south eastern Europe, southern Germany and Switzerland. Spelt flour was one of the very first wheats used to make bread. It became the principal wheat species in early Europe progressing to southern Britain around 500 BC.It has a tough husk, called a hull, which protects its nutrients. This stays on the plant right up to the time it is made into flour.

2. Wheat

Triticum Monococcum.[1] This is an early Wheat a grass widely cultivated for its seed - a cereal grain which is a worldwide staple food. Many believe is the old wheat that remains in cultivation today. Many wheat species make up the genus Triticum; the most widely grown is common wheat (T. aestivum).Wheat continues to be the grass widely cultivated for its seed, and has proved to be the world wide, staple food since the Neolithic period.

3. Oats

Oats are an annual plant, derived from a wild red oat and a common wild oat found in Asia Minor. Oats are suitable to grow in Britain and Northern Europe due to their cool wet summers, and has become an important crop for Northern Europe and Iceland.

Oats are well suited to the damp climate of Britain, which allows a winter sowing as well as one in spring - thus increasing the yield.

Evidence has emerged that people enjoyed their carbs even during the Paleolithic era - a period also known as the Old Stone Age -[1] that stretched from roughly 2.5 million to 12,000 years ago.

A new analysis of a Paleolithic pestle shows that it was dusted with oat starch, suggesting that ancient humans were grinding oats into flour and, presumably, dining on oatcakes or some other oat-based delicacy.

Below a list of fruit, vegetables and herbs that were found amongst Britons hedgerows and harvested by ancient Britons and Romans:[1]

Apple/crab apple, Malus sylvestris /Blackberry/bramble, Rubus fruticosus Bird cherry, Prunus cerasus, P. avium Cloudberry, Rubus chamaemorus Coriander, Dill Fennel Dewberry, Rubus caesius Elderberry, Sambucus nigra, Grape, Vitis vinifera Hawthorn, Crataegus spp.Sloe, Prunus domestica insititia, P. spinosa Raspberry, Rubus idaeus Rowan, Sorbus aucuparia Strawberry, alpine, Fragaria vesca Wheat, spelt, Triticum spelta Triticum aestivo-compactum.

Peas: a legume crop (these produce nitrogen in their root nodules) were introduced to the Romans and to Britain by the Aryans from the Middle East.

Wild cabbage: This was a favourite after the Romans conquered and settled in Britain. Native to Britain and Western Europe. These wild species remains closely related to the domesticated versions we see on today's supermarket shelves. With their domestication and their adaption to annual seed storage, planting, reaping, gave rise to Britain's early villages and hamlets.

Roman conquests of Britain The first Roman invasion and conquest was in 55 BC, when the Roman general, Emperor Julius Caesar, invaded Britain. The Second Roman invasion 43 AD, the Emperor Claudius resumed the work of Caesar by ordering another invasion of Britain under the command of Aulus Plautius, they landed in Kent with larger armies,, and went on to control Britons tribes in present-day south east England. They quickly conquered the remainder of Britons tribes and settled into Britons way of life

They quickly conquered the remainder of Britain and stayed until approximately 300 AD.

1. Ibid

2. V. Gordon Childe **Vere Gordon Childe** (14 April 1892 – 19 October 1957) 1936 Man Makes Himself.

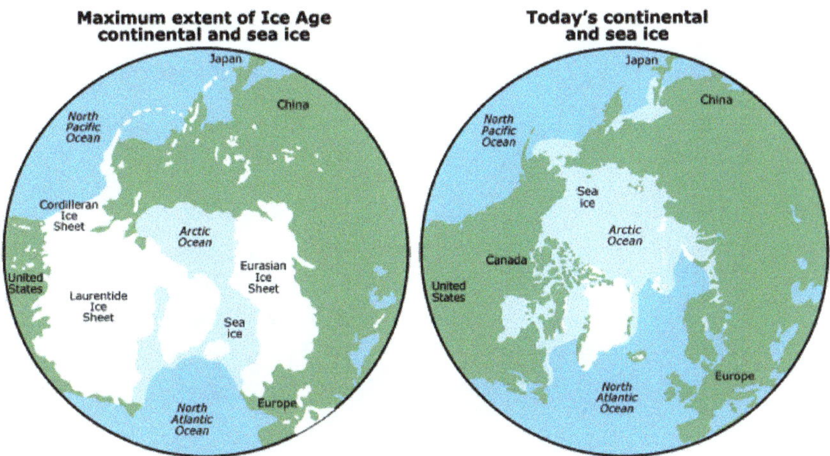

Historically the Laurentide ice sheet together with the Eurasian ice sheet covered much of the Atlantic from the United States of America to Europe.

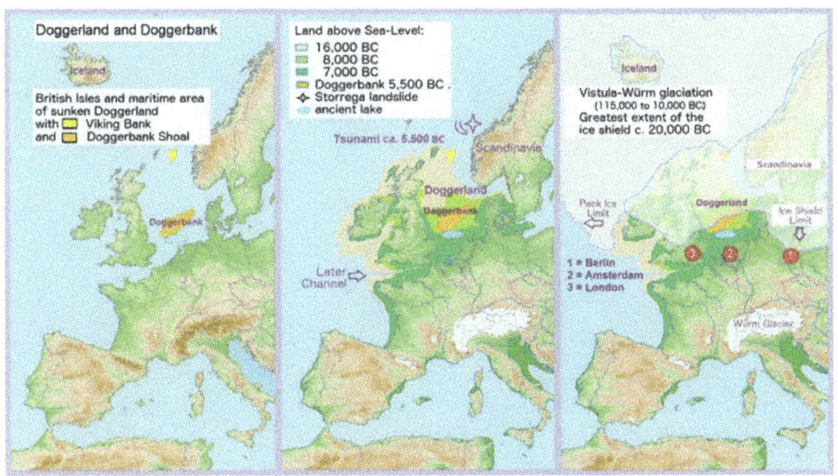

Extent of the ice shield illustrating land above sea level 20,000BC-5,5000BC.

Showing Inca hillside terrace farming.

The early farmers

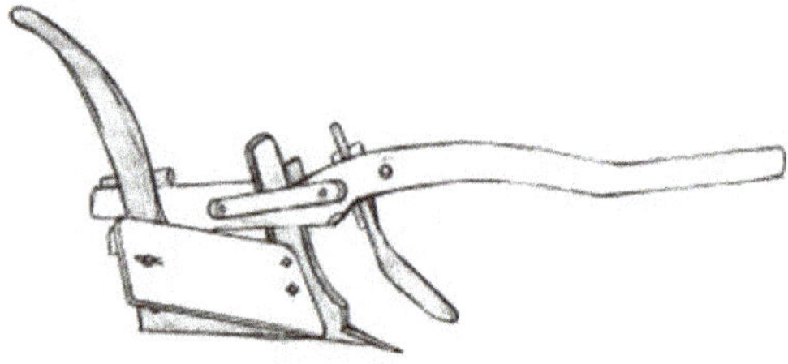

Primitive Neolithic and Roman ploughs.

The Neolithic era

The beginning of permanent settlement.

Iron age village life notice oxen working the fields

Stilted houses were built by fishing communities, living close to water, notice the canoe

Iron age early civilizations

Oxen working the fields, with a young boy sowing seed. Iron Age Round house showing early village life

Early humans beginning to farm

Iron age communities, built round houses

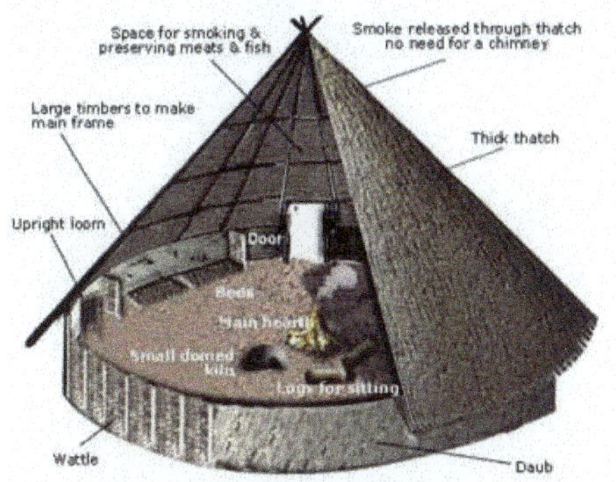

Inside an early round house.

Caves were still used in the iron age for families to shelter

Early iron age farmers cutting, thrashing stacking wheat.

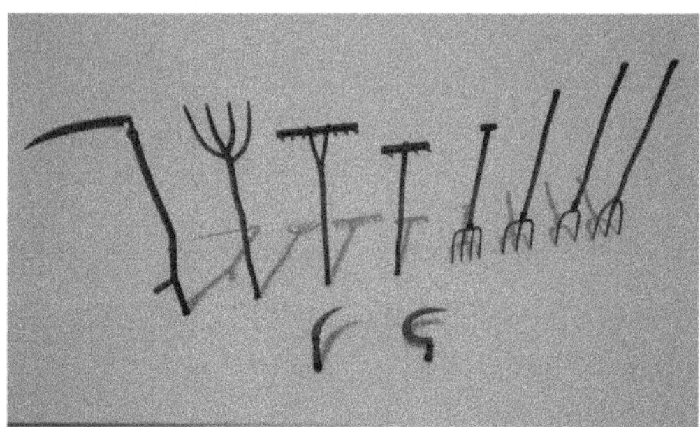

Hand tools illustrating, long handled, forks, rakes, forks, sickles.

An early plough, were often large antler bones.
A Roman is seen here working oxen making a furrow.

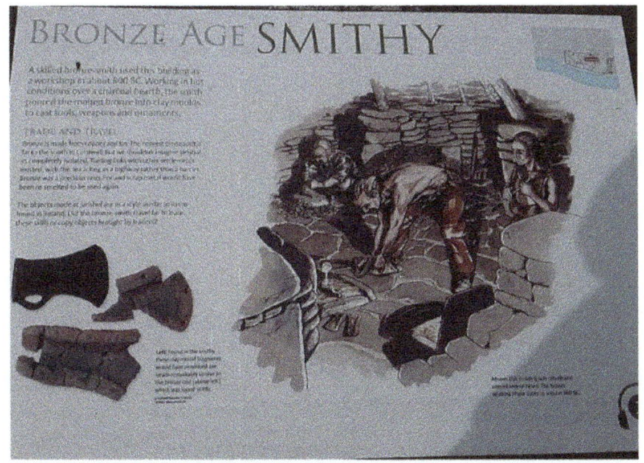

A bronze age smithy

An iron age kitchen

*Stone monuments, were sources of worship,
for early iron age humanities across the British isles.*

*Stone Henge the most important stone monument of this era,
still seen on the Salisbury plain in Britain*

Stone age rock outcrops, are still seen throughout Britain

*Large Ice sheet seen
over Greenland*

*Mortar and pestle stone used
for grinding corn*

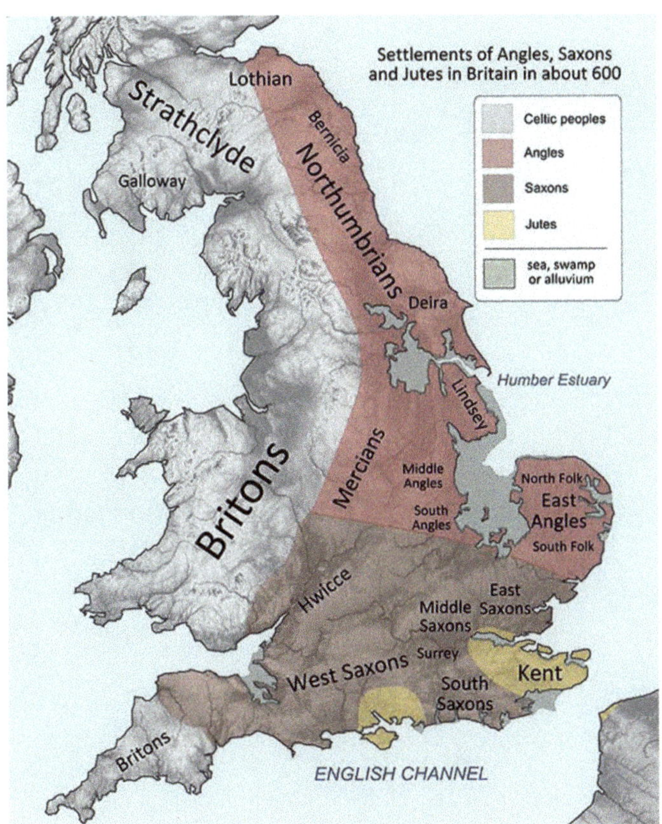

*Map of Britain with settlements of Angles,
Saxons and Jutes about 600 AD.*

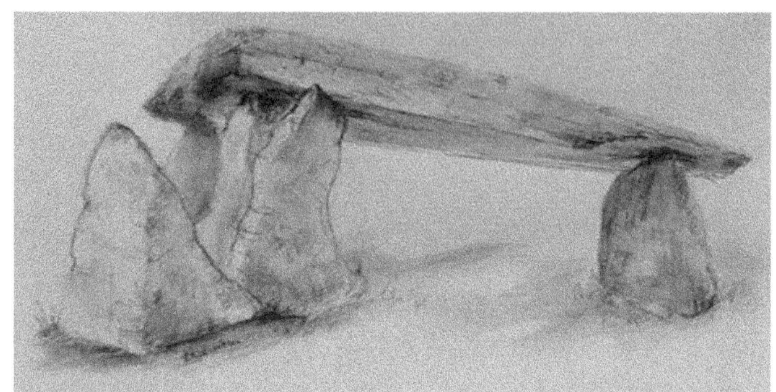

Pentre Ifan

Stone Henge

Mid Wales both are significant Stone Age monuments

Chapter 2

Roman Gardening
in Britain – 43 AD-410 AD
An Artistic Delight

Introduction

Britain's peasants in the 6th-8th century were made up of native Britain's, and the settled Angels and Saxons they became great gardeners of the age. In their gardens they began to grow the fruit herbs and wild vegetables they collected from Britain's hedgerows, many of which we still have today. They were not barbarians, but Germanic tribes coming to Britain from Central and Northern Germany. 1 Wikipedia, History on line

For the time the Roman's occupied Britain they began to write down and catalogue Britain's plants, giving Latin names to an extensive plant list. Latin plant names, we still use to catalogue plants today.

Majority of herbs and vegetables we use in our modern world, can be traced to back to the Roman settlement of Britain. The list includes maize, brassica', broad bean, carrots, spinach early peas, beet, kale, hemp, coriander feverfew, Rosemary, Thyme fig, lovage, parsley, poppy, peach, onion, mustards, pear, turnip, laurel, gladioli foxglove[1.]

The peasants along with the Roman settlers, began growing maize, with beans and a squash. They using a three-tiered system, whereby the growth of maize and supported a bean, with an early squash, growing up and entwining itself with the other two. This growing method developed into **Companion Planting.**

This chapter describes:

The period from 43 AD to 410 AD, when the Roman army gradually conquered and settled in Britain.

I describe the foundation of Roman gardening in Britain and how the Roman occupational forces found they had to rely on Britain's landscape to secure their hold over the country.

I record the beginning of crops grown by the Romans in Britain, in particular root crops such as beetroot, parsnips and carrots. These had been found growing wild in Britain hedgerows and were then domesticated by early Britons to grow in their hamlet enclosures.

The Romans introduced "madder"[1,] now regarded as an old English herb, used as a red dye. I discuss the importance of madder to Roman society.

The period 100 AD-300 AD became the foundation of Roman gardening and Britain's organic agriculture.

The Beginning of Britain's Organic Agriculture

The early British integrated themselves with the Roman occupying forces to form small farming communities, domesticating and cultivating wild seed such as maize and rye. As the tribes settled down into farming communities with the Romans, I believe this was the beginning of organic farming. The Roman's occupying forces were a great asset to the early British and were responsible for teaching them many gardening skills[1].

The Romans achieved a great deal during their occupation of Britain. They built a road system and aqueducts, many of which still exist today. Importantly they introduced a class system which is still in Britain to this present day.

The Romans introduced the term gentry and taught native Britain's a Roman way of life, how to wear their elegant clothes and live in better housing. They introduced the heated bath to their villas and improved many farming practices. The Romans lifted the lifestyle of all of Britain's population.

The Roman Garden

The Romans were first to establish the formal garden across Britain. They constructed an enclosed space around the settlements. They brought with them an understanding of climate and landscape from south-eastern Europe and the Mediterranean.

From 100 AD, Roman gardens were described as formal garden beds - symmetrical rows of trees and hedges shaped like a horseshoe. It suggested that the Roman garden was made to walk in, and shade loving plants - with pergolas with espaliered fruit trees and vines - were frequently grown.

Topiary was beginning to come into vogue with clipped hedges of all kinds of shapes. The Romans created gardens around their villas, with internal walkways, outdoor living pergolas, lawns, enclosed walkways and clipped hedging. In England, they used English box (Buxus), a plant native to Britain.

The Romans originally learnt their gardening from the Greeks and the Carthagians from northern Africa. The first horticultural manual was in fact from the Carthagian period (the Romans had conquered North Africa prior to settling in Britain).

Britain's Climate 100-300 AD

During this period, Britain's climate was unusually warm, as it was in most of Europe and the North Atlantic. While there is no written confirmation of this warmth, the evidence comes from tree rings and the mild conditions that allowed Hannibal to cross the Alps in 218 AD with elephants imported from Africa.

Roman Settlement in Britain 43 AD Onwards

Although Britain's Roman settlement was a gradual process, the occupying forces quickly learnt they had to control the Welsh border counties. Utilising the naturally high ground of the British midlands, they realised that this high ground became strategically important for their armies to control invading tribes from Welsh border counties.

During Britain's Roman occupation, the Welsh proved that they also had leapt ahead in growing plants. Approximatey 100AD a welshman by the name of Howell Dda understood the process of tree grafting.[1] (which I relate to in chapter 5). He understood that grafting was Thisonly possible when the cold winter had set in. This grafting art seemingly was brought to Britain via Italy by Syrian slaves.

The Romans also imported these slaves, knowing that they had the knowledge to tend to young plants. The money they earnt was often withheld until it was certain that the young trees had made a successful union with the stick and scion. When the fruit trees were grafted, there was an increase in their wage by 2 denarii every season. When the tree bore fruit, it increased by 3 dimes each fruiting season.

The Roman Currency

The Roman's produced their coin in the late 4th century BC and it continued to be minted for another eight centuries across their entire empire. Although the denominations for certain coins changed, the sestertii and denarii persisted throughout history. These two coins came to rank amongst the most famous and have become a guaranteed and widely recognised value through to modern times. They drove commerce, technological development and the exchange of all manner of goods and services. Throughout Roman society (as in our modern society) large currency payments could easily be made for large scale commercial activities.

Agriculture in Britain Under Roman Occupation

Britain's Roman occupation lasted for 400 years and changed British society and agriculture forever. The Romans introduced many cereal and root crops that we still have today - for example, cereals such as oats, spelt, barley, rye and wheat all owe their existence to Britain's Roman occupation, as do potatoes, turnip, leek, celery, onions and cabbage. Each hamlet farm had to supply a proportion of the food they produced to the Roman empire.

The Early Plough and Crop Rotation

*The Romans introduced an **Ard**, an early plough.*

This plough was pulled through the ground by oxen to make the soil furrow. They were not aware of the characteristics of Britain's soils and experienced many crop failures, due to natural soil nutrients becoming exhausted.

It took the Romans many years to learn to bring their domesticated cattle and other livestock into their nutrient deficient paddocks. They introduced crop rotation and root crops such as parsnips, beetroot and turnip were used to break up the soil. This was followed by leaf crops such as early cabbages, then cereals such as maize.

The early farmers allowed cattle to graze on the stubble of maize crops to naturally fertilise their soils. This led to the emergence of the three-field system that changed agriculture forever. Under this system, land is divided into three parts, of which one or two in rotation lie fallow in each year and the rest are cultivated. The villagers continued searching for food, finding wild cauliflowers and cabbages.

In the broad acre fields, the Romans experimented with cereal crops such as barley, lentils, and an ancient grain known as 'spelt'. They were the first to bring legumes, broad bean, wild carrot, (Daucus carota) and nettle (Urtica spp) into production.

The blackberry, raspberry and the sloe (used for making gin) are all now regarded as native to Britain. [1] The Roman's also grew and raised flax (Linum usitatissimum) for linen. Many of the ancient grains and hardy crops we take for granted today originated during this historic period. The Romans also brought ornamental plants to Britain, such as box hedging plants (Buxus), that are still grown today.

A New Garden

The Romans were responsible for the emergence of a new garden in Britain called the Persian Garden.[1] Roman gardens were grown around villas and consisted of formal flower beds, edged with small shrubs or box hedges. They were surrounded by pathways, water features and garden statues. The Romans also created small shrines and grew vegetables, herbs, flowers and fruit trees. In addition, they planted yew tree hedging and flowering cherries.

The flowers [1] included roses, oleanders, violets, crocus, narcissus, lily, gladioli, iris, poppy, amaranth and wildflowers. Sculptured box hedging and yew usually appeared in more complex gardens, along with plane and cypress trees. Roman interest in sculptured plants called 'plant topiary' remained in Britain for centuries.

Many of these Roman gardens are still seen today, laying the foundation for the gardens of the Renaissance period.

Britain's Roman Occupying Force

The Roman's finally left Britain around 380 AD – 400 AD, after which Britain fell into chaos. The Romans had to leave Britain to fend off Barbarian forces invading their homelands and to maintain control of their western empire. After leaving Britain's shores, the vast majority of the Roman army never returned. This signalled the end of the Roman occupation of Britain.

However, a few Romans stayed and made Britain their home, and continued to influence Britain's farming methods. They built new towns and had a significant impact on Britain's religion and reading. Britain's farmers, together with Roman settlers, converted more land for growing crops (primarily maize) and grazing. While in Britain, the Romans built vast aqueducts that used gravity to carry water to the populated areas and farmland. These aqueducts have lasted for hundreds of years.

The Beginning of Sustainable Agriculture

I believe that the Roman farming era in Britain was the genesis of sustainable agriculture. The farmers began rotating crops, with the addition of a green crop, and learnt how to use stubble to feed their livestock and naturally fertilise and care for their soils [1.]

The inclusion of green crop principles laid the foundation for the Middle Ages 'three field system', an innovation which changed agriculture forever.

Roman knowledge of creating a garden must not be underestimated. They may not have been very inventive people, but they gradually developed their gardening skills after conquering the Greeks and Egyptians. Indeed, they laid the foundations for many of the fine public gardens we are lucky enough to see around the world today.

Britain's Society and Economic Collapse

Caesar returned to Britain in 43 AD with much larger armies and landed in Kent. He found large areas of land under cultivation by native Britain inhabitants and Romans who had stayed and settled in Britain from the first invasion.

The Angle's and Saxon's and Dane's invasion and settlement of Britain (around AD 450) were the catalyst for the collapse of the Roman's British economy.

After the Danes left Britain, the country reverted back to small scale farming. The Romans who had stayed became part of Britain's society, creating the hamlets and villages we know today. They created domestic enclosures close to their homes that were protected against warring tribes by large ditches (dykes). This was an important development in the evolution of the domesticated garden.

Below is information on two herbs, *Weld and Madder,* which both played a critical role in early Roman and European history. [1]

Weld (Reseda luteola) (Common names include Dyer's Rocket, Dyer's Mignonette, Dyer's Weed, Woold and Yellow Weed)

This herb is mentioned in the bible and can be traced back to 1000 BC. It is one of the most ancient dye plants, still growing in Israel, across the Mediterranean coastline and throughout Northern Africa. The Romans introduced this herb using its red berry as a dye. They introduced the plant to Britain which grows up to

1.5 metres in height and has reddish-brown, fleshy, creeping and richly branched rhizome. Its flowers are small (2–5 mm across), yellow-green with hints of white, and are star-shaped with five petals. It flowers from June to August, followed by round, red-purple berries.

Weld is a biennial that undergoes an interesting transformation — from a large rosette in its first year to a tall spike in its second. After blooming, the foliage of the weld plant may turn the same pale yellow as its flowers.

Weld (pictured) was the oldest dye plant used in Europe, but ceased to be widely used by the end of the 19th century due primarily to the discovery of synthetic dyes.

Madder [1] (Rubia tinctorum)

Originally native to south-eastern Europe, the eastern Mediterranean, central Asia and North Africa, madder was introduced by the Romans to central and north-western Europe where it became naturalised. The plant can grow to approximately 1.5 metres in height, with long narrow evergreen leaves 6-10 cm in length. It is a perennial herb that climbs using small hooks on its leaves and stems.

Belonging to the coffee family, madder contains two organic red dyes, alizarin and purpurin. It is described as a moderately dull violet red. It is the most important source of 'true' red in plant dyeing. Madder root has been used as a natural dye for more than 5,000 years and was cultivated as early as 1500 BC. It was used as a colouring source by the Persians, Egyptians, Greeks and Romans, and was generally used for all red textiles before it was supplanted by synthetic dyes in the early 20th century.

Madder

The Role of Monasteries from the 9th–15th Centuries

With the retreat of the Roman armies from Britain, the country plunged into the dark ages. The Monks' gardeners had significant gardening knowledge and grew medicinal herbs, vegetables and fruit trees in some of the most famous walled gardens still on display today. All the monasteries around Britain were able to secure the best fertile soils and were self-supportive. [1]

One of the finest examples of a monastery garden that is still on display to the public today is the Bury St. Edmunds gardens that surround a Benedictine monastery dating back to the 10th century. In addition, a sketch plan of Christ Church Canterbury, dated 1165, remains a fine example of the knowledge the Monks possessed, while Abbey House Gardens in Wilshire England has over 1300 years of history, with the first king of England being buried in the garden.

Below is a short list of herbs and vegetables that would have been found growing in a monastery kitchen garden from the 11th century onwards:

Garlic, parsley, shallots, chervil, coriander, lettuce, chervil, savory, hyssop, cabbage, onions, leeks, celery, dill, poppy, radishes, corncockle, carrots, beets.

Fruit trees were also grown inside the monastery kitchen garden, including apples, pears, quinces, cherries, mulberries, medlar, grape vineyards (all suggesting that Britain was warmer at this time), peaches, strawberries, nuts, figs. [1]

Within the monasteries, kitchen gardens were situated under the shelter of a hill. For the northern hemisphere, kitchen gardens faced south for early season vegetable planting.

With the onset of the Protestant Reformation after Henry V111 came to the throne in the 15th century, many of the monasteries fell into ruins and were disbanded and destroyed.

There has been no change in the gardener's hand tools since Roman Times

The Roman Era

COMMON COINS OF THE ROMAN EMPIRE

Coins from the Roman Empire

Early wheat sheaf

The Norm n period 1000-1200

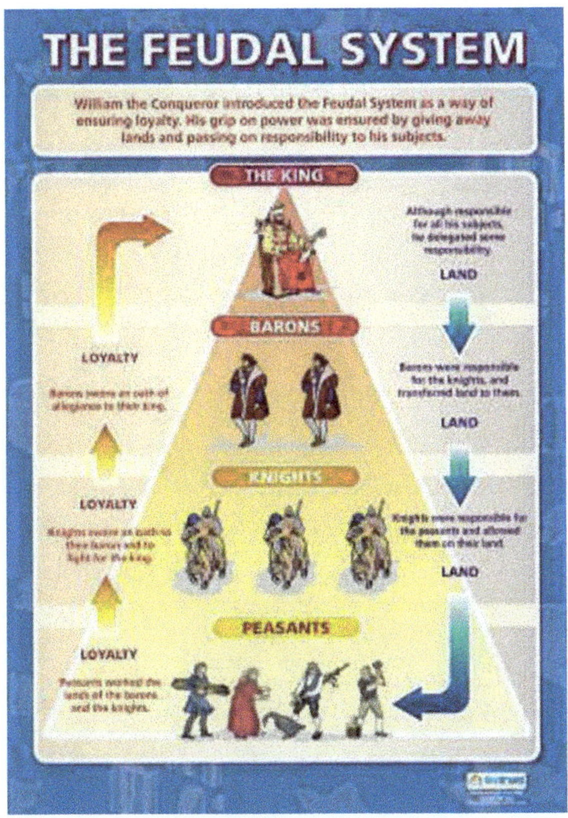

William the conqueror instigated the Feudal system as a way of ensuring loyalty and to keep his grip on power across Britain

The modern day sickle originated during the Anglo\ Saxon period

Scythes and rakes were used for grass cutting and raking, seen in the background a Norman castle.

The origin of a selection of modern day vegetables

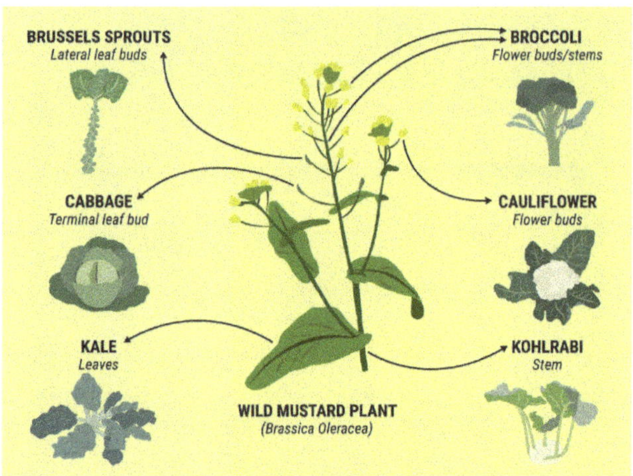

The wild mustard, is the original plant in this chart. The brussel sprout, broccoli, cabbage, kale, kohlrabi, all descending from it.

A Modern day cabbage, originated in iron age Britain

Peas collected from the wild in Britain, continues to widely grown by modern gardeners.

The pea was once picked from the wild hedgerows of Britain. It remains one of history's earliest vegetables, grown and domesticated during prehistoric times.

Simple Timeline
Of Human History

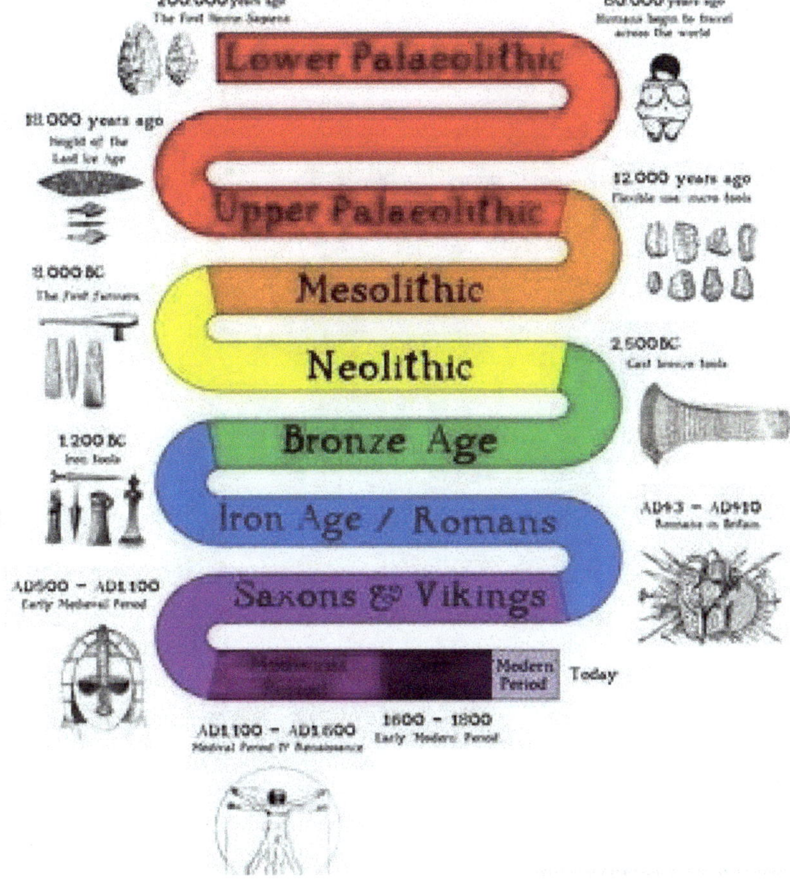

Early farmers with oxen pulling 'an ard' The farmer's standing on the plough to create more depth in the soil.

Round House village life: early farmers building hay stacks.

Chapter 3

Middle Ages Britain AD 900-1500AD

'Small scale peasant farming'

'Social upheaval / agricultural revolution / new knowledge/ catastrophe

Introduction

The medieval period in Britain took place approximately between 900AD until the late 1400 hundreds. It was a momentous period in World and Britain's history,

Firstly, the earth's climate under- went significant change, which resulted in horrendous social, economic, cultural unrest all across Britain and the northern hemisphere.

Secondly Britain had to deal with the retreat and fall of the Roman Empire, meaning they lost the stability and protection of the Roman armies,

There was significant amount of expertise in agriculture, social cohesion and road building, which the Roman occupying armies were responsible for, due to these social upheavals Britain plummeted back into primeval warring parties, also protecting themselves from invading barbarians, from Scandinavia.

In this chapter I focus on world's climatic and social upheaval and it's effect on growing food crops.

In medieval Britain it was the peasant farmer who dominated farming, growing crops using the three field system. Growing what crops he and his family could to survive Britain's severe cold weather.

The little ice age, during this period of the world history was due in part to an increase in sunspot activity, resulted in Britain and Europe plunging into a cycle of severe cold weather, that initiated Britain's Dark Ages, which was followed by a warming period lasting from the late 1400's – 1850's.

The role of the Medieval Monastery 1400's-1600's

The Monasteries with the Monks became the stable source of knowledge In astronomy, their knowledge of the stars and planets, gardening and horticulture.

Monastery gardens especially their "kitchen gardens' from the 5th century onwards shaped the beginning of organic gardening.

Two full time gardeners were often engaged in large monasteries growing a wide range of medicinal herbs, vegetables and fruit including apples, pears and plums in their orchards in a walled garden,. They scavenged Britain's wild areas, sourcing vegetable and herbs plants we take for granted today.

For example, their gardeners grew an early carrot, radish, colewort's, parsnip, leek, cabbage, garlic, onions shallots lettuce, parsley, dill, chervil, coriander.

The Monks became responsible for supplying food to the village communities and Lord of the Manor. They often provided lodgings and clothing to journeymen travelling throughout Britain ensuring they would survive Britain's harsh winters.

Monastery gardeners became vital members of monastery and outside communities. They used their herbs to treat the sick in their infirmaries;, They took flowers from the wild such as Cornflower, Daisy, Marigold, Rose, Poppy. They became pioneers of landscape art in particular 'topiary' shapes' we see in many public gardens today.

Note: Topiary is the art of shaping an evergreen or deciduous plant or hedge into different animal or bird shapes). English evergreen conifer Yew, or the deciduous Beech or Elm were widely used in the Monastery gardens. and are still used today.

The English Briar (wild Rose) originated during the 13th century amongst Britain's Hedgerows. Today hedgerows throughout Britain still have abundance of the wild briar. This wild briar rose over time became a " root stock" for many named Rose varieties we know today.

The Angels and Saxon invasion and settlement 6th AD onwards

While few Roman's and Anglo Saxon's settled, Britain remained a land of small villages, hamlets and emerging towns, around the monastery's, until the Norman armies under the direction of William the Conqueror invaded and conquered Britain in 1066 They used oxen to pull the plough and work the fields, animal dung was used to fertilize the fields.

The Doomsday Book

Immediately after conquering Britain William the Conqueror ordered a survey of all of Britain assets and population,. This he called the Doomsday Book it was commissioned in December 1085. England at this time had been at war with France so William needed to raise taxes to pay for his army. The Doomsday book (later called the Grand Survey) was introduced to raise land taxes from the lords of the Manor, and their serfs. There being additional taxes, on the number of serfs the Lord had.

Up until 1087 there was no knowledge of who occupied Britain's farmland and what crops and livestock they grew. The doomsday book became a record of 'land use and crops gown', this was the genesis of organic farming, together with the introduction of two farming systems.

The Doomsday book remains in public records office in London, national archives Kew Gardens.

At this time there were Two farming systems that changed the course of agriculture these were **the two field and three field farming systems,**

Firstly: I would like to illustrate the two field system.

Secondly: A three field farming system.

The table below illustrates the 'two field farming system'. which farmers used around the 8th century. It was a farming system that divided the land into two long strips. Farmers planted one strip of land with barley, or wheat (for example), while the other strip was used to graze livestock,(cattle or sheep) on the stubble from the previous year. Rye, pea, beans, onions were also grown in this two field system.

A two field system

	Field 1	Field 2
Year 1	Winter crop	Fallow
Year 2	Fallow	Winter crop
Year 3	Winter crop	Fallow

Secondly the 'Three Field System'

The three field system was a giant leap forward in organic farming, and remains so to this day. During the 13-14th century this farming system revolutionised farming for the next couple of hundred years. It involved a creation of a fallow plot, to graze livestock, on stubble from a wheat crop from the previous year. Their grazing naturally fertilized the paddock with their droppings.

This was the beginning of Organic farming, revolutionising Britain's agriculture that in time gave rise to the Agricultural Revolution of 16th century

A planning/planting of a three field farming system

	Field 1	Field 2	Field 3
Year 1	Winter crop	Summer crop	fallow
Year 2	Fallow	Winter crop	Summer crop
Year 3	Winter crop	Summer crop	Fallow

The three field farming system was a decisive advancement in farming production across Britain. It still exists today within organic horticulture, because it allows an Autumn planting of winter wheat, rye, the legumes peas, beans lentils, then potatoes, as the roots crop in the first two fields, while leaving the third field fallow. This too gave rise to companion planting, which over- time gave rise to increased yields. After harvesting nutrient hungry crops, farmers learnt Legumes peas, beans returned nitrogen back to the soil.

Introduction of ploughing

The three field farming system was the catalyst for trailing new mechanical inventions, bought about by the Industrialisation of Britain that began during the early 17th century.

Firstly there was the Watts stationary steam engine. This was a fine invention and an incredible piece of machinery.

A steam engine was placed at each end of the field to be ploughed, with a large rope attached to a wooden plough that in turn was attached to the engine. The engine pulled the plough through a furrow with a farmer's guidance. Once reaching the end of the row, the plough was attached to the rope to be pulled back by the other engine, at the other end.

The ploughing operations transformed farming, and machinery, into the age of the industrial revolution.

The beginning of farm industrialisation, assisted in increase of food production, which in turn improved Britain's food production, and increased European lifespan by 2 decades.

The Middle Ages climate change.

The Medieval warming period lasted from approximately 1000 AD-1200AD

After 1300 AD Britain and Northern Europe was subject to a severe cold period. This is thought to have occurred by low solar radiation, together with changes in ocean circulation and a heightened volcanic activity and the Samalas volcano on Lombok Indonesia erupting affecting the whole world's climate.

The Giant Samalas Volcano Eruption of 1257

One of the largest volcanic eruptions the world had ever seen was the Samalas Volcano eruption of 1257. This catastrophic volcanic eruption occurred on the Indonesian island of Lombok. The giant volcano caused columns of smoke to reach tens of kilometres into the atmosphere, burying Lombok Island, before crossing the ocean into Indonesia and onto to the Northern Hemisphere. This momentous volcanic eruption is thought to have been one of the reasons why the world entered a Little Ice Age.

This 1257 volcano, eruption has been recognized as the largest ever recorded, in ice cores in both Arctic and Antarctic ice sheets. Archaeologists recently determined a date of 1257-1258 as a mass burial of thousands of medieval skeletons in and around London·

Note: Tree ring samples show widespread summer cooling temperatures in the northern hemisphere, after the Samalas Volcano eruption

Medieval chronicles in Northern Europe document the occurrence of initial warming in winter of 1258, which is just following the eruption. This was followed by extensive wet and cold climatic conditions all through Europe. Extensive crop failure contributed to famine through- out Britain and countries in Scandenavia

Sunspot activity

Sunspot activity is a temporary activity, that has been observed continually since the 1600's. It's an eleven year cycle in the sun's activity, observed by sunspots on the sun's surface. A period of low solar activity ran from 1640's-1720's. This is documented as a similar time to the Little Ice Age

The Little ice age 1350's- 1850's

The little ice age resulted in Britain and Northern Europe experiencing severe cold weather coming after the medieval warming period, that lasted from 1000-1200 AD.

Today the intergovernmental panel on climate change suggest that The Little ice age was due to a gigantic shift in in solar radiation, volcanic activity, large variation in the earth's orbit, (orbital tilt) and a severe change in ocean circulation.

These natural phoneme's all undeniably contributed to the onset of the 13th century 'Little Ice **Age**'. Cooler summers were also experienced in southern hemisphere regions, too on the Australian continent and tropical Pacific

The severe cold weather that Britain experienced many traditional farming songs were written and special prayers appeared in farming communities to over- come the cold weather and foresee good crop harvesting.

1300-1500 AD life on the land continued to be a struggle. Vast glaciers and icebergs expanded southwards from Scandinavia towards Greenland and Scotland. The high rainfall and severe cold weather came down with glaciers expanding across the Arctic oceans and much of Britain lay under show and ice for much of the year.

Britain experienced torrential rain and deep snow for nine months of the year. Starvation became rampant, across Britain and Northern Europe which ultimately lead to Britain's "Great Famine" Britain had incredibly, high rainfall, sometimes over 300 inches in 150 days.

The meagre crops farmers did grow were often full of mildew, full of pests and diseases. 10 -15 per cent of people in England died. The cold weather resulted in Britain's Great Famine; bread became the main food staple. The severe cold weather persisted throughout the northern hemisphere for the remainder of the late middle ages. (14th-15th century)

This period gave rise to the Britain's Dark ages, with the onset of the Black Death of the 1300's.

The black death 1347

The Black Death was caused by "Yersinia Pestis", is a bacteria that was carried by the fleas in rats originated throughout the Himalayan Mountains and central Asia. The rats carried the disease, on merchant ships, sailing through the Mediterranean Basin, into Britain, and Africa.

The Black death symptoms, saw extensive rashes produced on human skin which eventually turned black, which later was confirmed as a plague. The black death was responsible for much of the unrest throughout Europe, eventually leading to war between France and England.

It was also the cause of monks leaving the monasteries, which resulted in the value of their land, greatly devalued.

As the population began recover, it is believed that one third of Britain's population died from the plague, the demand for labourers and free holders to work the farms was intense.

(in Britain's social structure Freeholders were peasants just below the Lord of the Manor,)

The Black Death a catalyst Peasants Revolt 1381

The peasants revolted, all across Britain due to the severe cold conditions bought about by the little Ice age and the taxes that were imposed by the King. They began by gathering under the leadership of Watt Tyler, and John Ball. These men led marches on London. King Richard 11, was finally compelled to negotiate. He finally promised land and the stop of forced labour.

Wat Tyler was later beheaded in the King's presence, with the peasants being persuaded to return home. It is a historical fact that many of the King's promises never eventuated.

15th-17th century late Middle Ages/Tudors

Now with the European climate returning to normal,…life on the land for the gardener and farmer slowly returned to normal.

The period of mechanical invention.

This was a time for vast improvements in **agricultural** growing systems (for example; three Field growing system) through- out Britain bought enormous social and economic improvements to Britain's population.

The three field system was the catalyst for the introduction of the mould board plough, which enabled farmers to move away from oxen pulled ploughs, to horse drawn ploughs.

However: there was still a problem with the fallow land within the three field system.

This problem was solved with the introduction of the root crop, which was trialled In East Anglia.

Root crops such as the turnip and swede were found they opened clay soils, that allowed drainage, and nutrients, to flow. The fallow land was no longer necessary.

The movement of labour into the ever growing cities, to work the up and coming cotton mills.

This was too a significant period of social change that companion planting played with the three tiers :Squash, Maize and the Bean. They were responsible for changing the way humans grew food. (The growth of Squash, and Bean were supported by the Maize)It was called the three tier system.

Although there is little written on garden's the serf's had around villages.

Madder and Weld found growing wild are Herbs now regarded as weeds.

Madder was originally native to South-eastern Europe, Western Asia, and North Africa, it was introduced to the Central and North-western Europe where it became naturalized. The Roman's introduced "Madder". Now regarded as a weed was regarded as a herb, used as a red dye, it is a perennial climber belonging to the coffee family (Rubiaceae). with tiny hooks on the leaves and stems.

Wood is a blue dye, cultivated and highly valued Madder is a plant originally from South-eastern Europe, Western Asia, and North Africa, introduced to the Central and North-western Europe. The Roman's also introduced "Wood"It Grows up to 1.5 m in height and has reddish-brown, fleshy, creeping and richly branched rhizome. It's flowers are small (2–5 mm across) yellow-green hints of white, star-shaped with five petals. Flowering from June to August followed by round, red-purple berries. The red berry the Roman's used as a dye. Roman knowledge of creating gardens must not be underestimated. Maybe they were not inventive people),they had picked up they gardening skills after conquering the Greeks, and Egyptians, but they laid the foundations for many of the fine public gardens we are lucky enough to see around the world today

A selection Vegetables and herbs grown in late Middle Ages – Tudor period

- Onions,
- Turnips, Parsnip, root crops
- Radish
- Lettuce
- Liquorice
- Mizuna
- Cabbage (Brassica's) Broccoli
- Leeks
- Asparagus

A short history on

Greenland "The Frozen continent"

The abandonment of Norse community living in Greenland was partially due to the severe cold conditions bought on the Little ice age(1400-1700AD. They disappeared sometime during the 14-15th century from Greenland's coast. A fact that remains a mystery, to this day. We do know however the ice shelf had expanded across northern Europe, Greenland, Iceland and Northern Britain. Theories do suggest they ran out of resources, the climate became too harsh, soils became sterile for the meagre crops they grew.

"No chapter in Arctic history is more mysterious than the disappearance of the Norse settlement.' Greenland's settlers "the Norse" had established two settlements, on Greenland with hundreds of farms and more than 3000 settlers at their peak".

History states Icelanders sailed to Greenland and found the island's western coast settlement had been abandoned, by the middle of the 1400 CE. The inhabitants on the Eastern Settlement of the island's southern tip were gone as well.

Many south coast abandoned settlements, are visible from archaeological diggings that are living proof of past settlements.

A short history of Greenland's settlement

It was in 986AD, Greenland's west coast was settled by Icelanders and Norwegian's. History states they had 14 boats led by Erik the Red. They formed three settlements – known as Eastern Western and southern settlements. [1]

They settled on Greenland's fjords near the top of the many islands. It became part of Denmark's rule from the mid 1250's. The Norse settlements, thrived for centuries on Greenland's coast, but disappeared sometime in the 15th century, due in part as history states to the onset of the Little Ice Age. Apart from some runic inscriptions, no contemporary records, survive from the Norse settlements; however some Medieval Norwegian sagas and historical works do mention a Greenland's economy.

There are Icelandic records that account for a life on Greenland in the 13th century. While later Icelandic settlements vanish sometime during the 14th and early 15th centuries. The abandonment of the Western and eastern Settlements coincides with the onset of significant climate change in this part of the world which began in the beginning in the late 13th century to early 14th century. This was in due partly to a decrease in summer and winter temperatures. Greenland's seasonal temperature varied significantly during the Little Ice Age, of the 13th-14th centuries, when it suffered a major decrease between of between 11 to 14 °F of maximum summer temperatures. The lowest winter temperatures of the last 2,000 years occurred in Greenland during the late 13th century. The Eastern Settlements on Greenland were likely abandoned during the little ice age sometime during this time.

Most of the residents on Greenland are Inuit, whose ancestors it seem to have migrated to Greenland from Alaska through Northern Canada. They gradually settled across the island sometime during 13th century.

Greenland is the least most densely populated region in the world, with modern Greenland having a small capital city named Nuuk on Greenland's Southwest coast with a population 56,081 (2020), the rest of the island is being very sparsely populated.

About a third of the population lives in Nuuk, the capital and largest city Greenland is now divided into five municipalities called– Sermersooq, Kujalleq, Qeqertalik, Qeqqata, and Avannaata.

Nuuk is represented by clusters of many rainbow-hued wooden houses.

They cling to a rocky outcrop at the mouth of a vast fjord. Three-quarters of Greenland is covered by the only permanent ice sheet outside of Antarctica.

Remains of Hvalsey church, a Viking part of the Vikings' Eastern Settlement in Greenland (occupied c. 985-1450 CE). The church lies near present-day Qaqortoq. A young couple was wedded at this church in 1408.

*Stone ruins of Hvalsey Church Greenland are all that remain of
500 years of Greenland's Norse" civilisation. The last remnant of the
Viking church at Hvalsey, in Eastern Greenland (settled and occupied
from 985-1450 AD) A young couple was wedded at this church in 1408.
The church lies near present-day Qaqortoq.*

*500 years ago Norse settlements on Greenland's South and West coast were
abandoned in early 14th-15th century. This was caused by the complete
depletion of Greenland's natural resources and severe cold.*

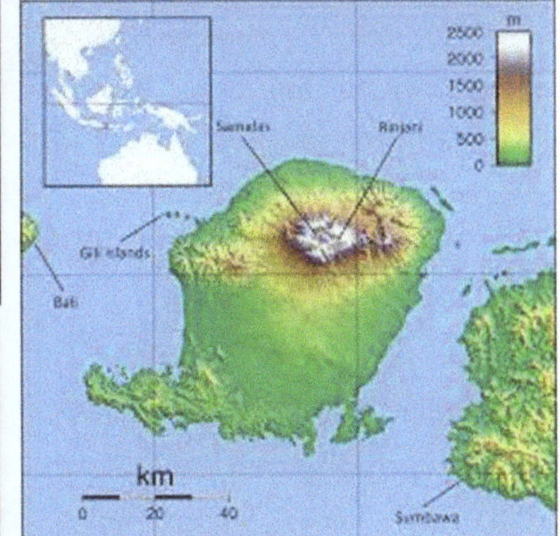

The Volcano Samalas in Indonesia erupted in 1257 was partly responsible for causing the Little Ice age, of the 12th-14th century. Indonesian eruptions of this era dramatically effected earth's climate across the whole of Northern Europe.

The little ice age in Britain of the late 1300's. These pictures illustrating the population coping with frozen temperatures. Life was cold and harsh when the little ice came to britain in the late middle ages, leading to the Plague and Black Death.

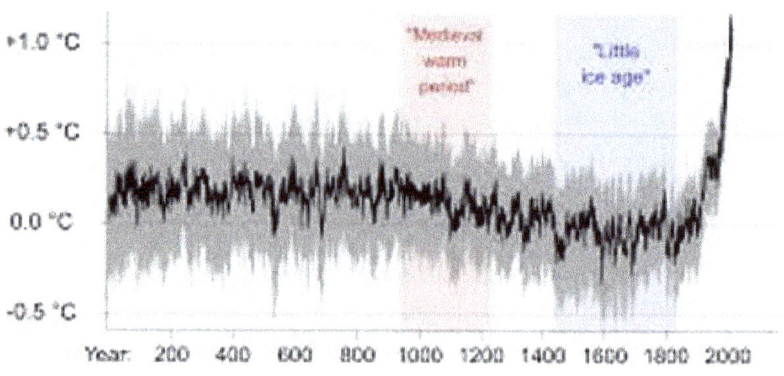

Climate -temperature chart illustrating the little ice age in Britain. Beginning around the 1400's and lasting until the mid 1800's.

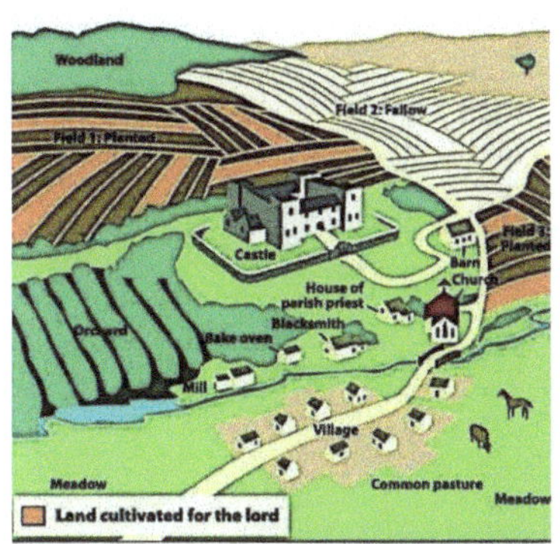

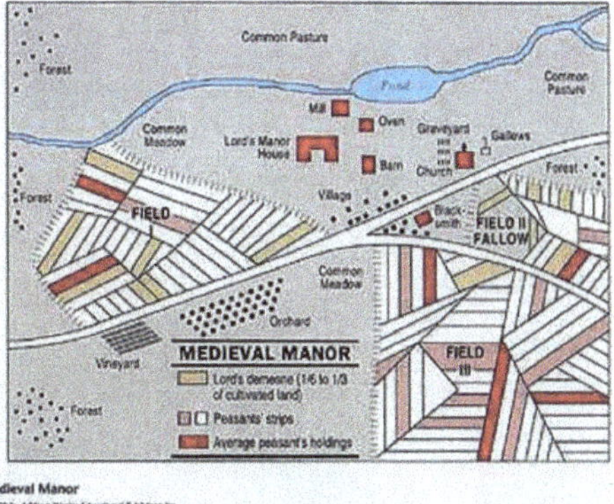

The three field system farming system was the most significant of this time. It allowed a fallow field every third year for cattle to graze, which in turn rested and replenished natural manures in the soil.

Peasant farmers working with a scythe, with the lord of the manor's house in the distance. The scythe was one of the most important of all hand tools, and is still in use in our modern world. It's curved blade is fitted at an angle to a curved handle. The scythe continues to be used for cutting grass.

The hand sickle is being used here to cut grass. Still one of the most ancient of harvesting and cutting tools. It has curved metal blade, attached to a short wooden handle. Still used in our modern world and throughout history this short handled tool was used to harvest crops or cut grass in stooped or bent positions.

The broad bean one of the ancient pod vegetables. Still found growing wild amongst Britain's hedgerows.

A bowl of fruit, all would have been grown in this historic time.

*Peasant farmer with a horse and early plough,
A Norman castle seen in the background.*

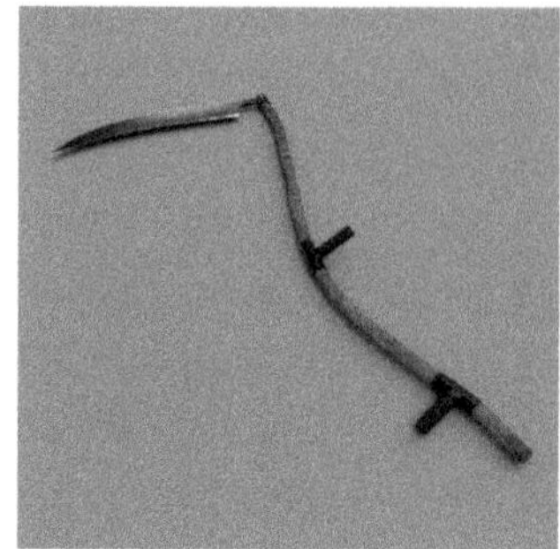

The scythe been in use since early Medieval Britain.

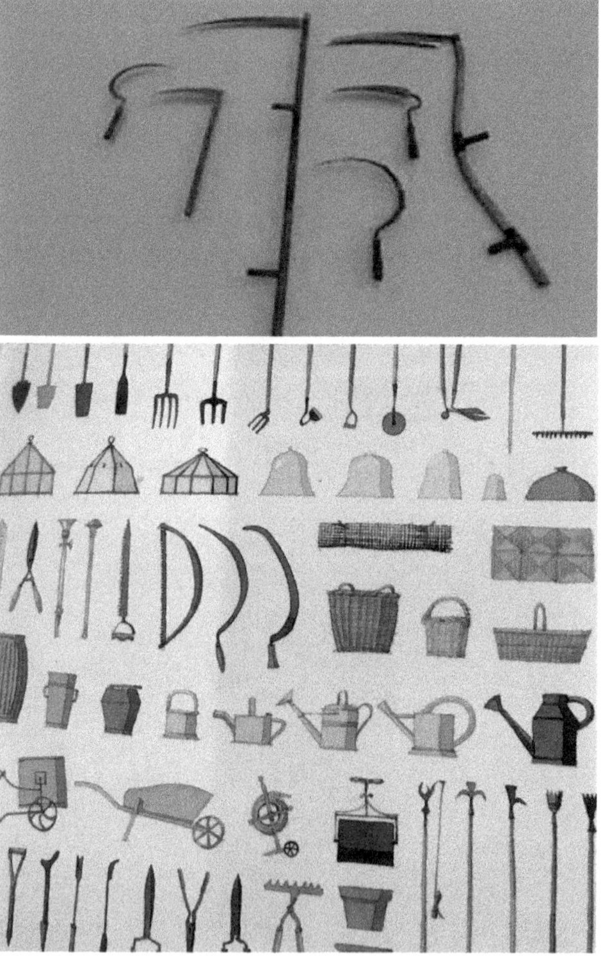

A collection of early medieval hand tools.

A plough from the early 1300's.

In ruins A Medieval monastery in present day Britain.

The little ice age was still very prevalent right through the middle ages to early the 1500's.on the land in particularly life was hard. Here icebergs floating down to the coast of Scotland

Chapter 4

The Agricultural and Industrial Revolution: 1500 AD – 1850's AD

This was an extreme cold period
in the world's history for the Gardener and farmer

Introduction

From the 16th-18th centuries, the earth continued to be in turmoil due to The Little Ice Age 'lingering on' throughout the northern hemisphere.

The Little Ice Age's extreme cold weather began after the middle ages' warming period, which corresponded to a period when the earth had no sunspots and lasted until the mid-17th Century.

At the height of the Little Ice Age, London suffered from the Black Death and the Great Fire of London 1666. However, as mentioned in the previous chapter, it is widely thought that Britain's and northern Europe's extreme cold weather was due in part to an increase in volcanic activity in Indonesia.

Stabilising of Earth's Temperatures

With Europe's climate remaining extremely cold, life for gardeners and farmers was harsh. Across Britain, they were just able to grow enough food for survival.

Peasants and small farmers continued working the land at least having control over what crops were grown. While landlords had minimal control over the cultivation of arable lands around villages, organic farming began to take root. Which became a major reason why Britain's burgeoning farmland from deteriorating due to overcropping and erosion. In his book, *Back to the Garden* (2015), James H.S McGregor calls this phenomena The First Nature.

As climates across Europe stabilised, the farmers and gardeners were now able to grow a range of root crops such as beetroots, onions, brassica cabbages, cauliflowers, early lettuce, and vetch (bitter lettuce). Vegetables arrived from America - including tomato, potato, and pepper - were also grown. In addition, farmers grew and stored grains, and kept cattle, pigs, sheep, chickens and geese. They also produced eggs and meat, and made clothing.

Britain's Industrial Revolution

This began with the exodus of labour from the countryside into Britain's cities. With the burgeoning population move to the cities, Britain's cities began to grow and prosper.

From the 16th century, the kitchen garden and large country estates came to the forefront, which began with landscaping of Britain's large estates

The 17th-18th Century Kitchen Gardens

From the late 17th century, gardeners and kitchen staff growing and preserving the fruit they grew in large, sealed bottles. Wild game was caught (pheasant, duck) and hung in kitchens to mature. Gardeners grew a wide range of medicinal herbs to make potions to cure aches and pains.

Apart from a few spices and sugar, all food for the community was grown by the gardeners and small scale famers.

Fruit became a staple diet, with apples, blackberry, gooseberry, raspberry and quinces grown across Britain's country gardens. Gardening and cookbooks were now being published. A typical recipe for a boiled beef stew included the ingredients of cabbage, carrots and turnips.

In the country house, the kitchen was the centre of the household (as it still is today). The housewife would find all the ingredients she needed in the garden. There would be a 'still room', where bottles were kept full of pickled fruit, onions, eggs and vegetables. There would also be herbal recipes and ingredients for cough medicines.

The Stuart and Jacobean Garden

In the 17th century, **landscape architects began designing famous** formal knot gardens **of the** Stuart and Jacobean **period which** emerged with a development of highly **formal** architectural style. These were comprised of the knot garden that sprang up throughout Britain's country homes. They were being influenced by elaborate French garden designers, who developed the term 'partiere'. They morphed into traditional square framed knot gardens. English Box (buxus) was the primary source of hedge material.

Throughout Britain's country estates, there was a heightened interest and understanding of how to create formal gardens. Controlling nature was at the forefront of the design of these large country estates. In this historical period, Europe was in turmoil as the Christians and Ottomans who fought for control of Europe. Growing crops still revolved around the three-field growing system, around a village community. Due to climatic extremes, there were good and bad years. For the peasant farmers, the ox and horse continued to be used to pull and carry. Animal dung was spread on the fallow fields, then planted with early pea, that provided nitrogen back to the soil.

It is important to note that farming was still at the centre of the community in the simple village lifestyle. Crops and a good harvest were prayed for in church and crop success was achieved using the *fundamentals of nature* (e.g., taking note of the time of year for sowing/reaping, looking after soils and ensuring village life was in tune with nature). This was also the age when gardeners and scholars began to grow herbs for medicines.

The Trigger for the Industrial Revolution

As mentioned previously, there was a great population shift from the countryside to Britain's towns and cities. This hailed the beginning of the Industrial Revolution. Britain now had a large unskilled labour force to run its factories and the invention of the stationary steam engine heralded the beginning of the mechanisation of Britain's farms.

Britain's factories demanded long working hours from their employees for a pittance of pay. The factory overseers were brutal men who demanded that workers work long hours and operate new mechanical inventions such as the 'Spinning Jenny'.

The Boulton and Watt Stationary Steam Engine

The invention of the Boulton and Watt stationary steam engine (patented between 1763-1775 with the Spinning Jenny) was a stimulus for the beginning of farm mechanisation and provided a catalyst for the foundation of the Industrial Revolution.

The stationary steam engine was used to pump water and power thrashing and reaping machines in agriculture. An engine was placed at each end of a field to be ploughed. A large rope with a wooden (later iron) plough was attached and pulled through the soil to create a furrow. This machine hailed the end of horse and oxen drawn implements, as well as the water wheel. The stationary steam engine was used to plough fields, operate seed drills, reaping and thrashing machines, and to pump water. It was also used to power cotton mills.

The next significant development was the 'sun and planet' invention. This invention replaced the water wheel and was the driving force of the Industrial Revolution, powering the cotton mills. Later models were used for pumping water and powering agriculture. The sun and planet gearing system by-passed the patent of the crank, patented by James Pickard. It turned the linear motion of an engine into a rotary motion and became the basis for rotating beam engines.

How it worked: *Picture: 'The sun and planet gearing system' was the motion of the beam around the sun (larger wheel), with a second rotating cog (smaller cog) fixed to a drive shaft which, in turn, produced a rotary motion.*

The Voyages of Discovery, Trading in Commodities and Slaves 1500-1600's

While Northern Europe was in turmoil, due to the French wars, and severe cold weather it was also the time of some major voyages of discovery, that began during the early 1500s, This was the time the Portuguese explorers began sailing their ships down to the tip of the African west coast, they encountered treacherous seas and soon realised that they needed stronger, sturdier sailing ships. With sturdier sailing ships, they began settling in ports down Africa's west coast.

Portuguese trade ships ventured into native ports stretching as far down to the tip of Africa's west coast. They soon began collecting natives, men, women and children who were traded as slaves from the 1530s onwards. It was in 1532 that the first slave ship reached Brazil which was then a Portuguese colony.

The slave trade eventually expanded throughout Britain and Europe. For the next three centuries, slaves were taken from the Africa's to the Americas and Europe, which was later called the Slave Triangle.

From 1722-1750s, Britain's agricultural exports accounted for 80% of total English exports, with over half of this amount being exported to America. In the 1700s, Britain's Atlantic exports to New England (America) were dominated by gigantic cloth markets, with cotton being brought in on trading ships from the West Indies.

This period also witnessed the dawn of great ocean voyages, with the coming of Regulated Trading Companies. To summarise:

- 1700 s -1850s, was the time of the Industrial Revolution.
- The agricultural revolution and the exodus of labour from rural Britain into the burgeoning factories became a catalyst for Britain's Industrial Revolution, which also became known as the 'Mechanisation of Britain'.
- New Inventions - the Spinning Jenny and the Watts stationery steam engine set the scene for the Industrial Revolution.
- The invention of new farm implements saw horse-drawn farm machines being replaced by machine driven ploughs, seed drills and reaping machines.
- Britain's Atlantic exports to New England (America) began with the gigantic cloth market of the 1700s.
- During the mid-1700s, Britain's agricultural exports accounted for 80% of total English exports and saw the beginning of Regulated Trading Companies.
- In the late 16th century, Britain and the Northern Hemisphere experienced severe cold weather, culminating in the Little Ice Age.
- After temperatures returned to normal, it was a time of the 'great gardeners' and agricultural change. The coming of the stationary steam engine and new farming methods giving rise to the 'agricultural revolution'.

Chapter 4

Supplement: The Inca Civilisation

The Inca civilisation was predominantly an agricultural society that farmed the high plateaus (3000m) of the South American Andes in the early 15th century.

The Incas used terraces around their cities to grow potatoes, quinoa and sweet potato. Their survival depended on growing food in the Andes meagre topsoils. Over time, the limited soils resulted in many crop failures. They soon realised that different crops could be grown in different altitudes, so diversified the crops between the coastal plains and the Andean mountains.

The terraced hillsides supported irrigation canals to slow or stop water runoff. This allowed rainwater to drain back to its source within the mountains. The terraces worked where land was scarce, the climate uncertain, and there was insufficient topsoil. To counter the climatic uncertainty, they also farmed coastal plains where they grew cotton, fished in the sea, and collected guano (the accumulated excrement of sea birds or bats) for fertilisation.

The Incas were also the first civilization to use proper hand tools for agriculture and had a high level of knowledge of soil conservation. Their diet was largely vegetarian, though they occasionally supplemented their diet with camelid meat (alpaca or llama) and seafood.

The Incas grew crops such as quinoa on the terraced hillsides where they introduced irrigation (quinoa is a vital protein and has returned to immense popularity). Quinoa was so vital to the Incas that it was considered sacred, earning it the name 'mother of all grains'. However, quinoa is not actually a grain - it is a seed. As a complete amino acid, it's a superfood and is highly rich in vitamin C and protein. It provided the Incas with the energy to work the fields at altitude.

Growing in abundance on the slopes of the high Andes mountain range, quinoa had a great significance in Inca culture as a food source, until the Spanish Conquistadores sent the native farmers to their Peruvian mines. Thereafter, non-native crops were produced for the Spaniards' consumption.

While the Incas lived on quinoa, potatoes and corn, they used many other plants for medicinal purposes. They also experimented with such techniques as freeze-drying potatoes - called chuño - without the benefits of modern technology.

The Inca's success and ultimate survival stemmed from the in-depth knowledge they had accumulated over hundreds of years about how to grow crops under harsh mountainous and arid conditions.

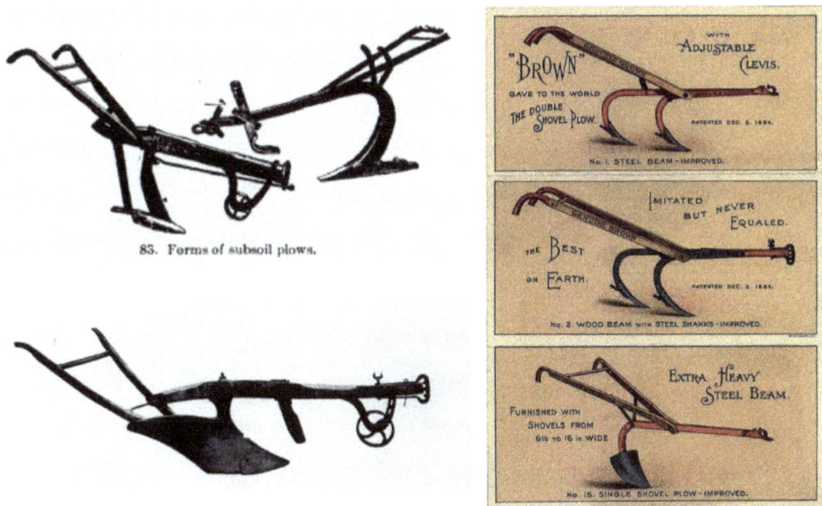

83. Forms of subsoil plows.

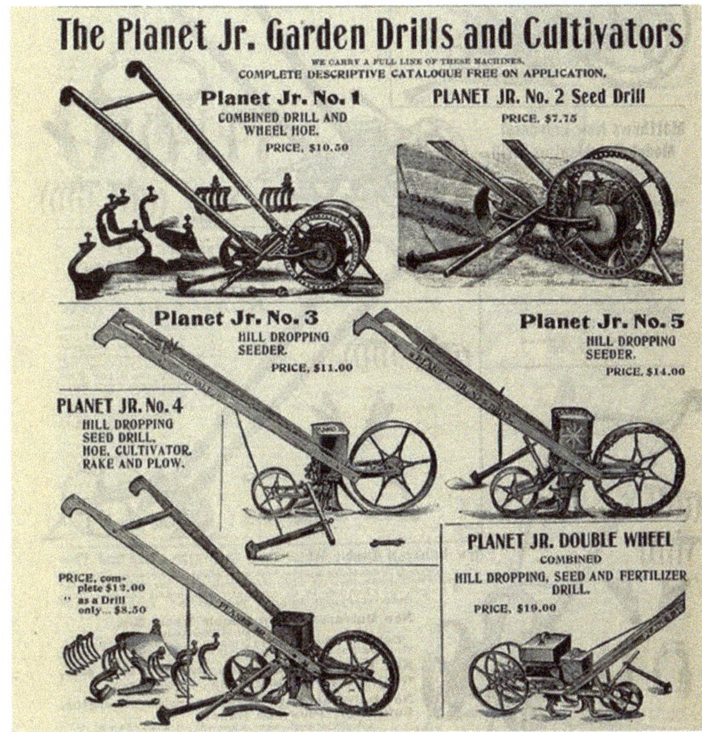

Forms of sub soil ploughs and seed drills from the early 18th century.

*Hidcote gardens here with the manicured beech hedges,
and box hedging(buxus) in Gloucestshire. Great Britain are a fine
example of a gardeners skill during the late 18th-19th century.*

Chapter 5

Influential Gardeners and Garden Writers

Tudor, Victorian period to modern day (1500's – to 20th century)

Introduction:

Throughout the Tudor historical period the little ice age was still having an influence on Europe's climate from the mid 1500's to the late 1700's. Britain and northern Europe continued to suffer from extreme cold. Rivers and lakes were frozen, agricultural fields were frozen and full of frost to a depth unsuitable for growing crops. It became extremely difficult to grow food for a growing population. Through horrific hardship Britain's farmers and gardeners continued to grow food needed to sustain Britain's population.

The foundation of plant propagation

The gardener and small farmer's knowledge of growing plants was vital for when Britain's and Europe's climate returned to normal temperatures, in the late 1500's. This was also the time that learned orchardists began the art of grafting fruit trees. (Simon Harward 1572-1614)

The tree 'whip and tongue graft', began in the late 1500's

Gardeners, nurseryman, market gardeners and orchardists began to learn the art of plant propagation.(taking plant cuttings and placing them into wooden trays with a refined garden soil mix.

> *NOTE: Nurserymen and growers had to wait until the mid 20th century for a soil compost suitable for growers and the nursery industry.*

> ### *John Innes compost*

> *In the mid 20th century a soil mix gave rise to the John Innes compost. During the 1970's this potting mix became widely used in the nursery industry. It used a soil, (later sterilized) as its main ingredient, mixed with a refined sand, and gravel. It remained popular until soilless potting composts (peat moss, fine gravel or washed sand) were established in the early 1970's)*

To propagate new plants Gardeners placed the wooden trays full of prepared cuttings into a glasshouse. In order, to prevent water evaporation they covered the glasshouse and trays with a crude sacking that created an ideal atmosphere for new plant roots to establish. The cuttings with the occasional watering showed they began to produce their own roots.

This eventually lead to a crude 'water misting system', which provided water to the leaf of plant. Eventually this gave rise to commercial cutting propagation methods which included seed raising and tree grafting. These propagation practises continue to be the mainstay of our modern nursery industry.

Gardeners and garden writers of the age

For the gardener and small farmer the 15th-16 century was a time of great change. I have chosen six writers whom I consider the most influential and facilitated significant change in gardening and horticulture over the centuries. Of course there are many more who influenced horticultural change over the centuries, however this is my list.

Simon Harward (1572-1614)

Simon Harward introduced plant grafting using the whip and tongue method. He also revolutionised the art of general plant propagation, which included cuttings and all other types of other propagation that included plant budding (a form of grafting a procedure done in summer, this involved taking a bud from a living plant and placing it into under the skin of a live plant called an "understock" normally at ground level).He also introduced Herbaceous perennial propagation, that included plant division, and separation.

Simon Harward began to illustrate his grafting technique in his book titled a 'New Orchard and Garden' it was published in 1631, focusing on planting and grafting fruit trees.

He understood and virtually created the 'whip and tongue' grafting practise, which involved joining the two cambium layers. He also learnt that keeping the graft wood cool and moist was vital for the graft to succeed. He knew a sharp knife had to be used to ensure clean cuts that exposed the cambium layer in each piece of wood was necessary to formulate the graft.

In his book 'A new Orchard and Garden' he also spoke of grading sorting, and storing apples, many varieties are still in production today such as Worcester Pippin and Permain, and Egmont's

Russet. He was the first to suggest that packing apples 'one by one' prevented bruising, in a box lined with dry straw, for cold room storage, this assisted in prolonging their 'shelf life'.

Now 200 years later, the midland counties and south East counties of Britain, Worcestershire, Herefordshire, Kent continue to be critical fruit growing countries.

John Claudius Loudon (1783-1843) Writer/landscape gardener/architect

John Claudius Loudon was a 18th century Scottish landscape gardener and architect. He went to school in Edinburgh, Scotland, and after leaving school he was an apprentice to nurserymen and landscape gardeners. Loudon moved to London in 1803 and became a very successful landscape gardener.

In 1806 he wrote an essay illustrating how he thought public squares needed to be designed and planted. His ideas remain important in designing today's urban landscape.

John Loudon was also a most influential horticultural journalist. In this era Britain was undergoing great landscape change from landscape architects such as Capability Brown, who designed over 170 parks, and Humphrey Repton, who was the last of the 18th century landscape architects.

The park and common

John Loudon became a famous gardener shaping early Victorian tastes in gardens and public parks he was the first to consider village and town public squares. Many of which we still see in modern day Britain. He wrote and published many gardening books with his wife, author Jane Webb Loudon (1807–58). Looking through many of his books, still available today, 'The Suburban Gardener and Villa Companion', is one of his best-known.

This a Herefordshire village, ending in Loudon's common

John Loudon landscape gardener to focus on the village green or common such this one seen in the Worcestshire Britain. He thought the 'common' in each town and village became vital for enhancing the wellbeing of the working population. Today thanks to Loudon across Britain we see almost every village, town, city, having good sized parks, and a common. This a Herefordshire village near the Malvern Hills, is a fine example of a Loudon's common.

By improving city and town planning, John Loudon concentrated writing on small gardens. of the 18th and early 19th century He became one of the first to develop an awareness and interest in public gardens and common park space. While many writers of this age focused on large country gardens and estates. Loudon wrote extensively on the skill of the gardener to grow vegetables and flowers, in the small suburban garden.

Throughout the industrial revolution and well into the 19th century Britain's cities were covered in smog, British working class lived in very poor housing, Loudon was determined to see them have access to a park or common all within walking distance from where they lived.

Loudon's Books and magazines

Loudon's first book on garden design was published in 1806 and was followed by many others covering all aspects of horticulture, landscape design and other related subjects.

He wrote an *Encyclopedia of Gardening (1822),* which included a plans for extensive kitchen and flower gardens that included hot houses, orchards, and gardener's lodges and offices. He then wrote *The Encyclopedia of Agriculture* **in 1825, and then** *Encyclopedia of Cottage Farm gardening*.

Loudon's introduced the first garden magazine a periodical devoted to horticulture. The full title was the **'Gardener's magazine and register of rural & domestic improvement'**. It was written, edited and published by John Claudius Loudon.

The magazine began in 1826, and was firstly published quarterly, which he increased its frequency to bi-monthly and then monthly, it ceased publication in 1844. He also contributed to other successful monthly gardener's magazines.

In 1828 he introduced a Magazine of Natural History and then an illustrated second edition of An Encyclopedia of Gardening in 1828. He then accomplished a major work for Britannica on fruit trees in an arboretum titled 'Arboretum et Fruticetum Britannicum published in 1838.

Loudon was definitely ahead of his time with magazines devoted solely to horticulture, his books helped shape Victorian suburban gardening, and were also the first to give extensive kitchen garden planning.

The Encyclopedia of Gardening

In his 'Encyclopedia of Gardening' Loudon emphasised the value of sustainability. He connected gardening theory with practice and the latest aspects of his time in all horticultural subjects (floriculture, arboriculture and landscape-gardening and design). In his gardening encyclopedia he included all the latest improvements that a gardener needs to know, and a general history of gardening from all European countries.

He provided detailed insights into the future of gardening, and what he thought a gardener should know during the 19th and 20th centuries.

Loudon's designs

In his garden design work John Loudon was definitely ahead of his time. He advocated irregular, picturesque gardens that were designed for botanical study, instruction and pleasure, as much as for innovative design. He was the first to call his style the 'Gardenesque'. Loudon's style became the dominant influence in Victorian gardens.

A famous piece of his work that that the modern world can be most appreciative of was his work titled '***Arboretum et Fruticetum Britannicum***'. This work was extraordinary in that it was published in three formats. With plates entirely uncoloured, and botanical details hand-coloured. Work began on this project in 1830, and was first issued from January 1835 and continued to July 1838. He included notes of the trees growing in individual gardens; did drawings of leaves, twigs, fruits, during summer, and the shapes of leafless trees, in winter. This piece of work became priceless for future gardeners, all over the British Isles. For its day his work presented an exhaustive account of all the trees and shrubs growing in Great Britain and their history, a remarkable feat.

Loudon's legacy

Loudon's legacy lives on firstly with Westonbirt Arboretum. History states that John Claudius Loudon was the first to consider and plant an arboretum. He was adamant that an arboretum, should be designed as a place where trees, evergreen and deciduous conifers and shrubs should be grown in the British Isles extensively for the purpose of observation and study.

Joseph Strutt a local philanthropist. ended up altering Loudon's plan to include a small botanical garden. He eventually added the wide range of tree and conifer avenues that we see today alongside plantings of low landscaped walkways.

The arboretum was eventually established in 1829 by Robert Holford and was extended by his son George Lindsay Holford. The British Forestry Commission took over the management of the park in 1956 and Forestry England in 2001

Today the collection of Maples (Acer dissectum spp) together with extensive collections of deciduous trees planted for Spring or Autumn colour, make Westonbirt well worth the visit when in the British midlands.

Loudon's legacy lives on with the Westonbirt Arboretum
Tetbury, Gloucestershire

Westonbirt Arboretum

Westonbirt Arboretum 'showing extensive under storey of Acer Dissectum (maples.) Upper storeys of autumn trees display the grounds for families to enjoy.

John Claudius Loudon encouraged Joseph Strutt to create the Arboretum at Derby, to show appreciation to the working people of Derby for the part they had played in helping him and his family amass his fortune.

Work on the Derby Arboretum Britain's second arboretum commenced in July 1839, and was completed in time for the opening just twelve months later 16 September 1840.

Derby Arboretum

Derby is one of the finest arboretum's in Britain, with many of its trees listed on the national register.

A catalogue of notable trees of Derby Arboretum are now growing through it's manicured grass are recorded by Britain's Forestry Commission.

Derby Arboretum

Derby Arboretum displaying it's glass houses with beds of annual colour.

Derby was the first publicly owned Arboretum, with John Claudius Loudon being responsible for a lot of its design. It will forever hold its place in the British landscape, as being the first, publicly owned, landscaped urban, recreational park in Britain.

Unfortunately there were many years of neglect, however in the 21 century now the Derby arboretum has been extensively refurbished. It employs many fine gardeners, and is on the English Heritage Register of Parks and gardens.

J Shirley Hibberd

J Shirley Hibberd was a gardening writer and publisher, from the mid 1800's. He wrote periodicals that included *'The floral world and garden Guide"* 1858-75. This was highly successful. He also wrote *The Amateurs Flower Garden and The Amateur's Rose and Green- house.* His focus was on plants he took out to plant in their natural role. He was the first to introduce them as objects of individual botanical study. He emphasised too that a gardener is to keep garden top soil loose and have an understanding of adding manures which were congenial for plant growth. He knew that a gardener must become proficient in all garden tools.

By the end of the 18th century, flower gardening was becoming popular and employing gardeners from Britain's urban working class. Britain's large cities and towns all had allotments now growing a mix of flowers and vegetables.

Vita Sackville- West 1892-1962, Professional gardener, novelist, journalist

There are extensive writings on Vita Sackville West and the influence she had in the early 20th century on garden design and the horticultural industry. For the purpose of my book I want to do a short resume of her influence, on the gardening and Horticultural industry. With her husband Sir Harold Nicolson she created Sissinghurst, in Kent during the 1930's. Her husband designed the strong structure the landscape needed, which provided the strength for the innovative informal plantings, she experimented with room enclosures with the creation of the white and rose garden. The study of single colour gardens remain one of her best achievements.

With the advent of the 20th century, we must thank these innovative gardeners and writers for their contribution to the gardening profession.

Gertrude Jekyll 1843-1932 A British Horticulturalist, garden designer, writer

Gertrude created over 400 gardens, across Britain, with one of her most famous Munstead Wood. Her influence in modern times within the gardening industry cannot be underestimated. She was an avid writer, with over 1000 written articles published. Her own gardening books are still widely read, with many having been updated. She contributed to Country Life with upwards of 1000 articles being published. Edwin Lutyens was her supporter, over many years. She collaborated with him on many garden designs and the practicalities of working in her gardens.

Edna Walling 1895-1973

Edna was born in Britain in 1895, however was regarded as Australia's own. She was an avid gardener, conservationist, and writer.

Markdale and Kiloren in Crookwell NSW are two of her best known gardens she designed in 1947. In the 1940s Walling was a household name, across Australia with her popularity she became a house hold name.

kiloren near Crookwell, was a windy hillside when Edna Walling saw potential of the site to create a garden

Markdale near Crookwell is often regarded as Edna Walling's finest garden. She created and used the 'HA HA wall' that exaggerated and did not inhibit the amazing view of the surrounding countryside.

She published four successful books which include:

- *Gardens in Australia* (1943);
- *Cottage and Garden in Australia* (1947);
- *A Gardener's Log* (1948); and
- *The Australian Roadside* (1952) Garden magazines and Nursery catalogues.

In the early 20th century early garden magazines, the Gardeners Chronicle, The Garden, and The Field together with fine Nursery catalogues, provided excellent references for flower, plants, trees, shrubs and vegetables. Hillier's Nursery is one example that produced their manual of trees and shrubs, and proved to be valuable reference for growing trees and shrubs.

Note: A gardener's hand tools, haven't changed for a millennium

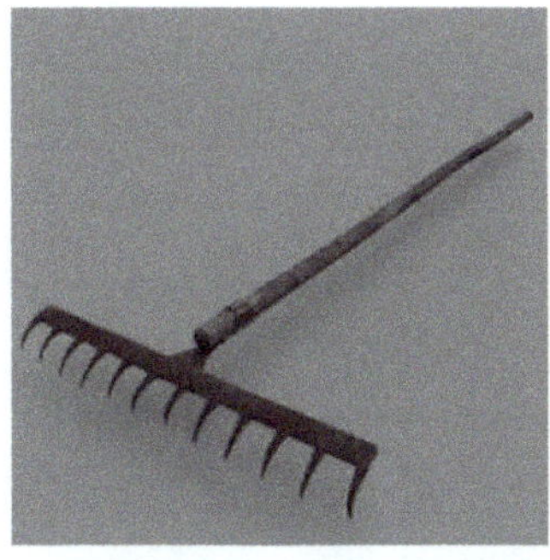 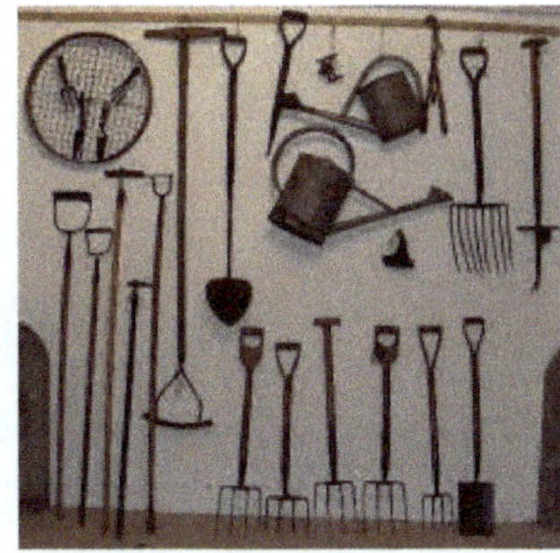

Hand tools: rakes, sythes, syckles, watering cans and garden sieves

Modern day gardener still care for their soil and plants using these hand tools that have not changed since Roman times.

I include now an extremely rare book first published in 1597. It was enlarged and amended by Thomas Johnson in 1633, and reprinted in 1636. Gerard was noted botanist of his time. It was called :

"Leaves From Gerards Herbal" by John Gerard.,

The following illustrations describe John Gerrard's view of garden plants. He wrote following the text below that; *gardeners are manifold creatures of God none have provoked men's studies more, or satisfied their desires, so much as plants have done*

'Among the manifold creatures of God that have all in all ages diversly entertained many excellent wits, and drawn them to the contemplation of the divine wisdome, none have provoked mens studies more, or satisfied their desires so much as plants have done, and that upon just and worthy causes: for if delight may provoke mens labor, what greater delight is there than to behold the earth apparelled with plants, as with a robe of embroidered worke, set with Orient pearles and garnished with great diversitie of rare and costly jewels? If this varietie and perfection of colours may affect the eie, it is such in herbs and floures, that no *Apelles*, no *Zeuxis* ever could by any art expresse the like: if odours or if taste may worke satisfaction, they are both so soveraigne in plants, and so comfortable that no confection of the Apothecaries can equall their excellent vertue.'

John Gerard

Reflections by John Gerard from his book "Leaves From Gerard's Herbal" published in 1923, with arrangements by Marcus Woodward. He was one of the first to give a practical guide to the making of a home garden, growing flowers, fruit trees and vegetables for home use. His description of the gardener is interesting.

John Gerard begins with

"A small garden area should be well prepared, with every effort should be taken to prevent the land from becoming crusty, and hard". He understood a soil's capillary water action, for the plant to uptake water, to pass off water into the atmosphere, and the flow of nutrients that assisted with plant growth.

At this historic time, he also gives an excellent description of the duties of a gardener

Below are three extracts from his book I have included:

1. Sweet Marjerome 2. Ginger 3. Wood Sorrell

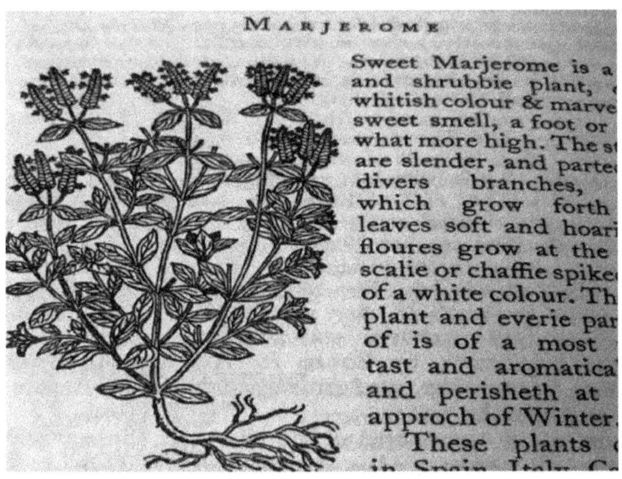

Sweet Marjerome (sweet Marjerome), a herb with a sweet smell, and whitish colour

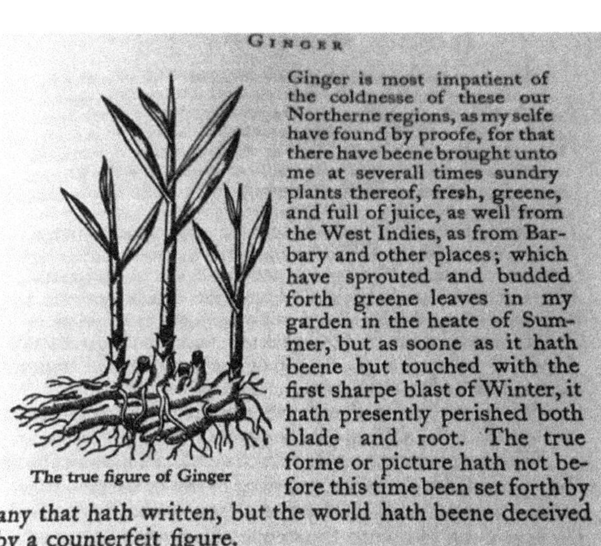

Ginger The most important herb from the West Indies. Not suitable for coldest of climates.(he says that ginger was impatient in the coldest of regions)

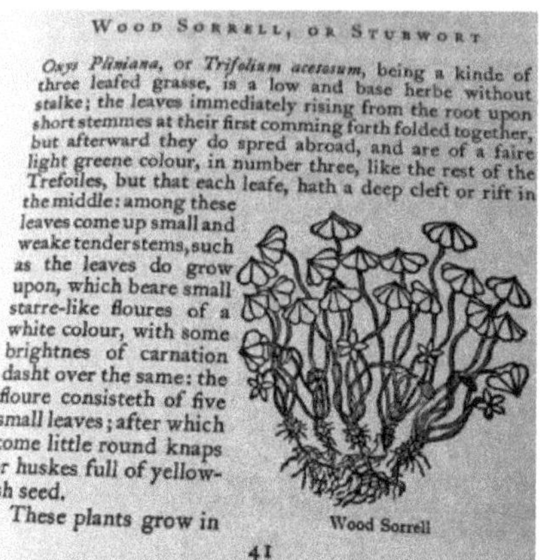

Wood Sorrel. This is a sort of three leafed grassed herb. Gerrard however recognised that there is no stalk with its leaves rising immediately from its root base.

Horticultural Advancements from 1830's

'The Plant Nursery and landscape industry'

From the 1830's onwards plants were now able to be transported much more easily back to England, with regular ocean voyages, from the sub-continent and the new world.

This also meant botanists were able to examine plants that were being imported from all over the world, and now able to raise their own specimens.

From the 1830s onwards hybrids and plant diversity was also increased with experiments in laboratory gardens. The most famous one was at Down House in Kent, where Charles Darwin investigated the action of earthworms in the soil. He also did a lot of work with orchids, and how they adapted to fertiliser.

The 1830's was a time of patenting 'Horticultural inventiveness', with for example the first lawnmower was patented in 1830. In

1840's Britain's glasshouse industry took a giant leap forward with the development of sheet glass in 1847. Sheet glass meant that large glasshouses could be built much more cheaply. Asphalt was also invented in the in the 1860s. Gardeners helped lay the"asphalt"paths at Broadsworth Hall garden in Yorkshire.

In the 1840's gardeners became valued and learned members of the Horticultural and landscape industries.

1860's a classic Victorian style glasshouse.

In the 1860's glasshouses such as this one seen here were made possible with the invention of sheet glass. The glasshouses were made predominantly with an apex slanting roof, coming down to vertical sides. An innovative way of fixing glass to timber was invented, that meant glass was fixed using a clip fitted to timber frames. This created large glass sheets transported maximum light into the house. The whole of the glasshouse was supported by a brick foundation normally approximately 900-1.2m high.

In the picture above cold frames are seen as an addition to the Glasshouse. Cold frames (as they were called in the northern hemisphere)are areas gardeners, and horticulturalists, placed their rooted cuttings in trays to 'harden off' to establish their roots.

The Victorian Era in Britain rein of Queen Victoria beginning on June 20th, 1837 until her death in January 22nd, 1901. was one of significant change politically, socially, and religiously. There were massive advancements in science, technology, and engineering, more that the any other era in history had witnessed.

Britain's "Golden Years" (1850-1870) called by historians, with increased industrialization, farming, and gardening initiatives' all led to a growth in the national income. However there still great poverty, with children still in factories and down mines. Life on the land growing crops was still extremely harsh. Around the world there was peace abroad and at home.

The period later known as the Mid-Victorian era, was the period of calm, with agricultural, social and economic advances.

The "Victorian garden, became well established with landscaping of Britain's large country estates. The likes of Capability Brown proved that landscaping Britain's country houses were for the common man not just for Britain's royal family. This was a period when large country estates were landscaped all across the British isles.

Towards the latter end of the 18th century, social changes within Britain's middle-class, enabled them to have significant purchasing power, to buy their own vegetables and fruit, as well as grow their own. The affluent members of Britain's society were able to build and landscape large country homes and gardens such as Croome in Worcestshire seen around Britain today.

Croome Worcestshire

Horses was now used on the land, for a wide range of farming activity including ploughing, mowing, and seed sowing. They were also hitched to trailers laden with produce such as straw bales.

By the 1860's farm labourers and their family lived in a thatched house, attached to the farm. The thatch roof of this cottage is in bad need of repair.

87. Spring-tooth harrows.

18th century horse drawn farm harrows and crop seeders were used extensively, right up to the 20th century

From the late 18th c apples were grown as espaliers on walls. Apples are being picked grown on an espalier system.

Westonbirt arboretum

The flowering cherry tree paddock, in Weston Arboretum supports spring flowering bulbs.

Westonbirt arboretum displays, many varieties of maples, elms, and chestnuts great collections of autumn colour trees.

Westonbirt arboretum's Cedar trees illustrating a large snow fall.

Britain's forestry commission *As England's largest land manager, we look after more trees than any other organisation. Our forests provide amazing place s for people to enjoy, for sustainable timber to grow and a home for wildlife to roam.*

What separates us from other organisations is that we're always adapting; from cultural changes over time to bigger issues like a changing climate. We are developing forests today while carefully planning the future. It's a job that never stops growing.

Blenheim palace, Winston Churchill's family home

Autumn colour maples feature in the gardens of Winston Churchill's family home. This is, one of many significant gardens in Britain, employing many professional gardeners.

*Formal Rose
gardens*

*Benheim palace lake,
and conifer garden,
with the summer
house seen on the
lake forshore*

*Old parliament
House Canberra
The formal rose
garden, during the
1980"s*

*Many professional gardeners, tended to these rose gardens. This picture is
of the Senate rose garden taken in 1985*

Formal hedged gardens

Many skilled gardeners maintain these large formal hedged gardens seen in the next three pictures. The hedge in the background is formed by 'pleaching' (partly cutting back their tops, and laying down the branches to form the hedge).

The late 18 century the cottage garden, was becoming popular, onions, leeks, leaf crops, planted in symmetrical patterns, allowing for gravel pathways

Gravel pathways feature here with brick edging in this cottage style vegetable garden. Gardens are bordered by box hedges, supports in the gardens allow for climbing vegetables, such as climbing beans

Professional gardeners were highly sort after in the late 18th century with the advent of these large glass houses. With many sailing ships returning to Britain with exotic plants, from the New World, many large glasshouses were built to tend to the new plants.

The Gigantic Volcano eruptions in Indonesia were responsible for the change in climate during the middle ages. This resulted in severe winters, and was partly responsible for the Plague and the Black Death throughout northern hemisphere, during the late middle ages.

When a garden belongs to an historic property or listed building a glasshouse can also be made to a design that complements those all-important period details, from decorative embellishments such as cresting and finials to the pitch of its roof. For keen gardeners possessed of deep pockets, it can even be custom-built to a shape, size and design that fits seamlessly into an awkward site or to replace an original period glasshouse that's long beyond repair.

Chapter 6

The Victory Garden 1939-1945

A Victory garden "A personal memoir from Kathe aged 84 world war II"

1943-4: How I Became Addicting to Gardening in World War II

In World War II, some 15,000,000 Americans served in the armed forces. Unfortunately for my super-patriot father, his broken eardrums and poor eyesight meant he was categorized as 4F and no armed service – not even the Seabees – would accept him to serve. To compensate, my civil engineer dad not only constructed rail spurs and built railway bridges in his full-time job with the Delaware & Hudson Railway as it accessed raw materials for the war effort in the Adirondack Mountains in upstate New York, but also worked part-time at a newspaper (doing everything from writing to delivering, the newspaper) and a veggie shop to cover for more able-bodied men and women away in service. And, during the couple of years we lived in a very small northern tier town while he and his team built a bridge, he, my glamorous mother and I won a prize for the 'Most Productive Victory Garden in North Creek'.

The US Victory Garden campaign announced in 1941 aimed to engage the 'home' population in the patriotic effort to raise vegetables and fruit to avoid rationing. The program created almost 2,000,000 gardens - "from suburban backyards to small city plots" - and "provided 40% of vegetables grown in the country during the war".

I am 84 now and am still active in a large-ish garden. My two inspirations are my French-Italian grandmother's huge WWII vegetable garden, barely contained by cottage garden borders filled with bulbs and seeds painstakingly ordered during the winter from Burpee's Catalogs which she farmed virtually alone (well, I had the job of chasing the neighbours' cows out of the corn now and again) and my mother and father's huge Victory Garden. My dad's quirky sense of humour shows me in a photo, aged 7 or so, standing in front of a v-shaped farm implement, reins draped over my shoulders, implying that my parents hitched me up to dig furrows in our prize-winning Victory Garden. Those were the days!

Digging for victory

During the war the "Digging for victory"(1939-1945) was a growing practice that Britain put into place to ensure all waste and spare land was used for growing vegetables. This included Railway edges, embankments, and all vacant land around Britain's country towns and villages. They were all turned into vegetable gardens growing crops such as potatoes, beans, onions, peas, leaf crops to help the war effort. This was basic organic vegetable growing which was taken up by approximately 18 million gardeners around the British Isles.

Many Posters were printed this one explains the 'Digging for victory' scenario.

While Britain was fully involved in fighting the war many supply lines came under threat from German U boats. It became imperative all across Britain, local councils, ornamental gardens and lawns and even sports fields and golf courses could be requisitioned for farming or vegetable growing. Instead of mowing school sports fields sheep were seen grazing there. By 1943, the number of flower and vegetable allotments had doubled to 1,400,000, including rural, urban and suburban plots.

BBC radio programmes "In Your Garden"

The second world war was the time BBC radio produced a popular gardening programme called *In Your Garden* with C. H Middleton(22 February 1886 – 18 September 1945). Middleton was the first really popular radio personality, reaching millions of listeners keen for advice throughout the war on gardening. Cecil Henry was another British gardener, writer and together with C.H. Middleton they were two of the earliest radio and television personalities and broadcasters on gardening for the BBC.

Middleton's broadcasts in Britain during the 1930s and 1940s, were especially important in the campaign "Dig for Victory". In his time on radio he offered many practical responses to assist with food rationing.

The launch of the Victory garden:

An extract from Your Victory Garden:" *Since we have entered the war, in 1939, we have been able to supply our population with enough food to keep strong, and healthy, and to keep our industries producing machines at top speed. Now as the war is reaching a*

critical stage, our population has relied on canned ration food. It is the fresh vegetables that are grown by our gardeners, that will keep our population healthy, and active. Britain has almost 18 million families, we will meet their needs of fresh vegetables, by growing victory gardens, as we approach a critical time of the war everyone needs our help. In particular on the farm; in suburban gardens and back yards; in school gardens and in community gardens"

As war broke out across Europe during the late 1930, it became obvious that the vast supply chains of fresh food coming into Britain came under threat from the many German U boats now patrolling the English channel and the North Sea. To compensate for the shortage of food for Britain's population, vegetable and flower gardens began to be planted, all across Britain. These were later called 'war gardens' or 'victory gardens', and by 1943 over 20 million gardens across the British Isles were producing 8 million tons of fresh vegetables per annum.

On a personal note, I remember, in the 1950's our village in the British midlands beginning vegetable allotments. I remember my parents still having ration books, which had to be stamped with every vegetable, or meat purchase. Allotments sprung up alongside our railways sidings and roadside verges.

Vegetables allotments/ railway embankments

This was also the period that parcels of land were awarded to railway workers to grow root crops especially, parsnips, carrot, onion (in 1939 onions were in great demand), and leaf vegetables alongside Britain's rail tracks. To this day we continue seeing vegetable allotments adjacent to Britain's rail lines. My grandfather worked for British Rail and had a magnificent vegetable allotment garden alongside our local train station. Britain still had severe food rationing well into the 1950s which meant new homeowners still had to grow their own vegetables. To this day, the rail sidings continue be a vital link between the community growing vegetables and the provision of produce for local markets and horticultural shows.

An amended Allotment Act.

Passed in 1950 this act established an advisory body recommending that four acre blocks be set aside per 1000 head of population.

The allotment vegetable garden

The allotment vegetable garden was highly productive in terms of land use. They accounted for 1.3 million plots that produced over 1 million tonnes of vegetables. They continued to play a vital role in the supply chain after the war with allotments growing such as onions, beetroot and parsnips, runner beans, broad beans, green peas, kale, cauliflowers, cabbage, potatoes, carrots, brassica and vetch. History states that the normal allotment size was approximately 250 square metres. 'Locally Home Grown produce was shown at all the' Horticultural Shows throughout Britain from the 1950s. onwards. One of the largest was The Three Counties Show covering Herefordshire, Worcestershire and Shropshire. They were a showcase for livestock and, importantly, organically grown local produce from local farms and allotments.

The Allotment Decline of the 1970s-1980s A steep decline in allotment vegetable gardening was due to the ever-increasing need for suburban housing. In modern Britain, there are still provisions for allotments to be made available, but waiting lists are common due largely to modern day concerns chemically altered food stuffs. Spare open field paddocks, were turned into large vegetable gardens. Poultry, cattle and sheep were raised on the 'common' within the village. Local apple and plum orchards too came into production, all to supply the local greengrocers, and the butchery. My father had a magnificent vegetable garden, of nearly half an acre, growing, potatoes brassicas, root and leaf crops.

Of course the local food supply was designed to take the pressure off the public food supply bought about by the war effort. They also created a lot of personal satisfaction to grow something. These gardens produced as much as 40% of the nation's food during the war, and well into the late 1950's.It goes without saying that all these vegetables gardens were grown in the pristine rich organic soils, with no chemicals or artificial fertilizers used at all throughout the British isles.

As America joined the war in 1941, there was a massive food effort, that touched all the population. In large towns and cities all across the USA people ploughed their front and back yards. They began to grow massive amounts of vegetables for the war effort.

Two are really worth mentioning: Firstly public land was put to use in San Francisco, with the lawn at city hall and around the Golden Gate, being ploughed to grow vegetables. These vegetable gardens became some of the best in the country. Secondly on the East coast of America in Boston, their common was ploughed up for vegetable growing.

With the research that has been done for this chapter, it reinforces the beginning of modern day organic vegetable growing. It began with the independence from corporate Victory food systems to the beginning of community vegetable gardens growing a wide selection of food crops.

Here we see the beginning of "the victory vegetable growing handbook" offering suggestions.

"The handbook offers suggestions the Victory garden" offering suggestions for a victory garden.

Describing common errors growing vegetables, including waste seed, excess fertilizer.

This handbook offers some suggestions to those who are leading the great drive for Victory Gardens, and points out certain things to watch out for — common errors which waste seed, fertilizer, land and labor, and therefore must be most carefully avoided in wartime.

What is a Victory Garden?

During **World War II**, Victory Gardens were planted by families in the United States *(the Home Front)* to help prevent a food shortage. This meant food for everyone!

Planting Victory Gardens helped make sure that there was enough food for **our soldiers fighting around the world**. Because canned vegetables were rationed, Victory Gardens also helped people stretch their ration coupons *(the amount of certain foods they were allowed to buy at the store).*

Because trains and trucks had to be used to transport soldiers, vehicles, and weapons, most Americans ate local produce grown in their *own communities.*

Many different types of vegetables were grown-such as **tomatoes, carrots, lettuce, beets, and peas**. Victory Gardens were responsible for bringing Swiss chard and kohlrabi onto the American dinner table because they were easy to grow.

At their peak there were more than 20,000,000 Victory Gardens planted across the United States. That was one Victory Garden for every seven people!

By 1944 Victory Gardens were responsible for producing 40% of all vegetables grown in the United States. More than one million tons of vegetables were grown in Victory Gardens during the war. That is the weight of 120,000 elephants OR 17,000 army tanks!

People with no yards planted small Victory Gardens in window boxes and watered them through their windows. Some city dwellers who lived in tall apartment buildings planted rooftop gardens and the whole building pitched in and helped.

Many schools across the country planted Victory Gardens on *their school grounds* and used their produce in *their school lunches*.

The U.S. government printed **recipe books** describing how to prepare **home grown vegetables** to make nutritional and tasty meals. Agricultural companies gave tips on how to make seedlings flourish in different climates.

Excess food grown in Victory Gardens was *canned and used during the winter months* to help supplement the amount of food available.

Growing Victory Gardens gave Americans on the Home Front a feeling that they were doing something helpful to win the war *(and they were)!*

THE NATIONAL
WWII MUSEUM

THE VICTORY GARDEN,

A SERIES OF PICTURES OF GARDENER'S DO AND DON'T IN 1942

The following 6 pictures is a series of pictures showing gardeners in 1942

"Dos and Don'ts to grow vegetable Gardens

Picture 1 The great drive for Victory Gardens

COVER PAGE These series of pictures offer directions of what was on offer to gardeners during the war years in 1942

Picture 1 'Garden opportunities on the farm', in the community garden, School yards and back gardens

Picture 2 Gardeners and Their Opportunities

Picture 3 Gardeners planting a mixed Vegetable Garden in 1942

Picture 4 1942 Gardeners had to focus on seeds, fertilizer, and soil

Picture 5 'This is War Work' in 1942

Picture 6 In 1942 this series of pictures illustrate a dozen don't for gardeners

This is a sample of the handbook that gardeners in 1942 had to focus on through wartime

This handbook offers some suggestions to those who are leading the great drive for Victory Gardens, and points out certain things to watch out for — common errors which waste seed, fertilizer, land and labor, and therefore must be most carefully avoided in wartime.

Gardeners' Opportunities on the farm, in community gardens, in school gardens, and backyards

Here are the opportunities

On the farm.

Every farm where weather and water supplies permit can produce the family's entire year's supply of vegetables, both fresh and processed, and also as much fruit as possible.

In town and suburban back yards.

Families who have sufficient open sunny space and fertile ground can grow a large supply of vegetables for their own use.

In community gardens.

People living in metropolitan areas seldom have enough suitable ground at home for a garden, but supervised community projects with space allotted to each garden have proven successful. Preferably they should be within walking distance or a short bus or street car ride. In some towns and cities, groups have arranged with a nearby farmer for the use of an acre or so of good land to use as a community garden, paying in either crops or cash. As part of the bargain, the farmer plows and drags the soil.

In school gardens.

Rural and city schools can have gardens planned and managed on a scale that will provide a large part of the fresh and processed vegetables for school lunches.

Picture 3 GARDENERS PLANTING A MIXED VEGETABLE GARDEN IN 1942

16

A small garden

Beans, snap (pole)	½ pound seed	After harvesting beans, follow with 3 rows of turnips; 1 ounce seed.	
Beans, snap (pole)	½ pound seed	"	
Beans, lima (pole)	½ pound seed	"	
Beans, lima (pole)	½ pound seed	"	
Tomatoes (staked)	2 dozen plants		
Tomatoes (staked)	2 dozen plants		
Carrots	2 packets seed	After harvesting, follow with late plantings of beans, beets, lettuce, turnips.	
Beets	1 ounce seed	"	
Kale	1 packet seed	"	
Turnips	1 packet seed	"	
Cabbage	30 plants	"	
Onions	1 pint sets	"	
Radishes	1 ounce seed; 2 half-row plantings, 10 days apart		
Spinach, New Zealand	¼ ounce seed		

50 feet long (along the north or west side) and 30 feet wide.

Picture 4 1942 Gardeners had to focus on seeds, fertilizer, and soil.

Only real soil can turn a plan into produce —

Don't let a Victory Gardener waste labor, seed and fertilizer on the usual built-up or chopped-off city yard. Under the thin layer of sod will often be found nothing but clay or debris. But, don't suggest chemical analysis, which would take too long and is seldom necessary. As a simple test - if it grows a fine crop of flowers or weeds, it's soil. Caution anyone against planting in the shade of the old apple tree, or in any other shade.

About 8 inches is deep enough for plowing - too deep, if subsoil comes up. Small gardens can be turned and broken with a spade or fork. Large gardens should be plowed with horse or tractor power. Community gardens should arrange for a complete plowing and dragging before planting time.

It nearly always takes fertilizer —

Good soil plus fertilizer equals the foundation of a garden. Plenty of manure is the best answer, or manure plus a commercial fertilizer. If commercial fertilizer is used without manure, it is necessary to keep up the organic content of the soil with leaf mold, compost, or similar material. Have new gardeners consult one with experience or a bulletin for satisfactory methods of preparing the soil.

A special Victory Garden commercial fertilizer will be available this year through arrangements made jointly by the Department of Agriculture and the War Production Board. It will be available in 5 to 100 pound packages and will contain 3 percent nitrogen, 8 percent phosphoric acid, and 7 percent potash. It must be used only for production of food, never for ornamental plantings. It will have a ceiling price.

Seeds must not be squandered —

Impress on each gardener the importance of buying only the seeds called for in his garden plan. If all gardeners are careful, there will be enough seeds available for every garden. Careless buying and use of seeds is unpatriotic.

A common error is wasting seed by sowing too thickly. Pea and bean seeds should be spaced as the plants are to stand, never thinned later. Beet and chard "seeds" produce several plants each, allowing later thinning. Small seeds in general should be sown about 3 or 4 times as thickly as the final stand expected, and thinned as they grow.

Detailed information on planting will be found in State Agricultural College bulletins on gardening.

6

Picture 5

'THIS IS WAR WORK' In 1942

In 1942 Britain was in full swing in producing food, for its population. The nation reinforced that food is what sustains life. Their farmers managed to record crop levels throughout the early 1940's.

This article reinforced the fact that Britain's families grew over 18 million' victory gardens'. Many needed help, as it was the first time they had planted a vegetable garden.

This is war work

As a nation, we have always taken food pretty much for granted. Not the farmers, of course. Food is the stuff life is made of, to a farmer. But the rest of us haven't always understood that. We have always had the idea in mind that there was plenty of food, if we just had the money to buy it. Now we are learning that a nation or a group of nations is no stronger than its food supply. We have stopped taking food for granted.

When we were attacked by the enemy, the nation had on hand splendid stocks of most foods and fibres, and our farmers were in a position to increase their production. We were able to throw this wealth of food ammunition into the battle for civilisation.

Since we entered the war we have been able to supply our civilians with enough food to keep strong and healthy and to keep our war industries producing at top speed; to supply our fighters throughout the world with the heavy diet they need; and to provide our allies part of the food strength they need to keep fighting. We intend to see the job through, and to help the starving victims of oppression get back on their feet as we free them.

Our farmers produced a record amount of food in 1940, then broke that record in 1941, and the 1941 record in 1942. Their goals are still higher in 1943, but civilian and fighting demands keep mounting, while farmers must make out with less labor and less replacements of machinery and equipment.

As the war nears the critical stage, we find fewer canned goods on our grocer's shelves. This just can't be helped. Malayan tin supplies have been cut off, and much of the tin we have must carry food to the battle fronts. Furthermore, with trucks and railroads so desperately overworked, it is a miracle that food from distant points reaches your grocer as regularly as it does.

People who have always relied largely on canned food now realize that their canned goods ration allotment will not feed their families, and that the fresh vegetables their grocer is able to get will often fall short of demand. This situation is a special challenge to parents, for children especially need a regular diet of vegetables to keep strong and healthy. We understand now better than ever before that adequate nutrition is the bed-rock of the nation.

About 18 million families this year will meet the situation by growing Victory Gardens. Many of these people will be growing a garden for the first time - and they need help.

1

Picture 6 in 1942 this series of pictures illustrate a dozen don't for gardeners

A dozen dont's for gardeners

1. Don't start what you can't finish

Before you plant a garden, count the work involved even before seedtime and through to harvest. Abandoned gardens are a waste of seed, fertilizer, tools, insecticides, and labor.

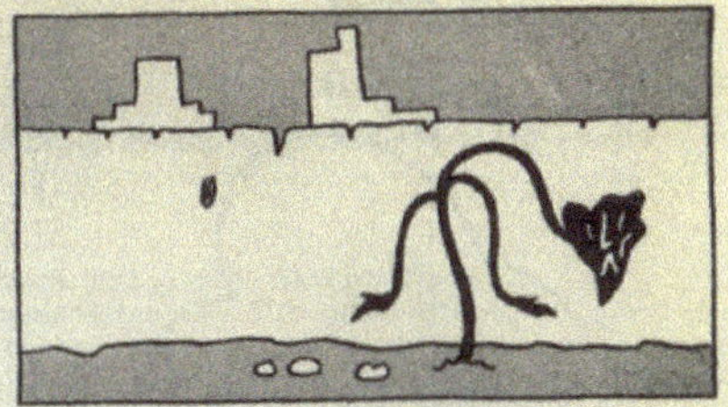

2. Don't waste good seed on bad soil

Gardens need good, well-drained soil, not the usual kind of city lots where soil is mostly cinders and rubbish. Places where weeds flourish are promising garden spots.

3. Don't work ground too soon

Starting too early will spoil the soil. When a piece of earth will crumble apart as you hold or press it between your fingers, the soil is dry enough to cultivate. Make sure yours is.

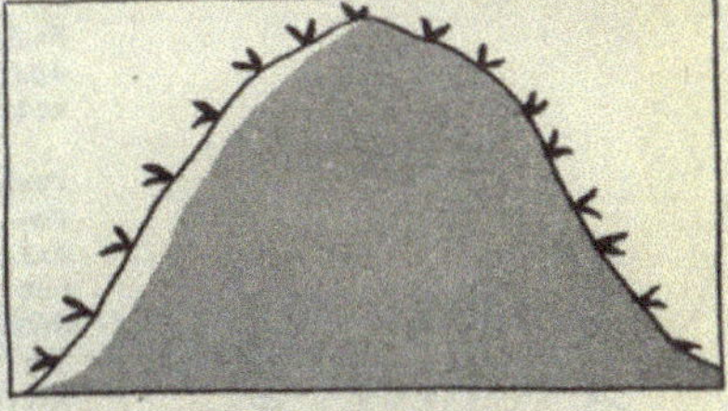

4. Don't run rows up and down a hill

If you must plant your garden on a hillside, make sure that the rows are horizontal along the side of the hill. If you plant them up and down, rain will wash off seed and topsoil.

5. Don't use too much seed

Crops seeded too thick will come up close together, they will need lots of thinning. Learn how to space the seed you use. Overseeding wastes seed and labor. Waste won't win.

6. Don't plant too much of one thing

Too much of any vegetable, even if it comes from your own garden, is hard to take unless you are sure someone else can use the surplus you can't use. Plant a variety of things.

14

CONSUMERS' GUIDE

7. Don't let the pole beans black out the beets

In fact, don't let any of the tall crops shade the short ones, whatever they are. Growing things must get sun. Plant climbers, like beans, to the north; short ones, to the south.

8. Don't wield too heavy a hoe

Vegetable roots grow near the surface. They are tender, too. When you cultivate them deeply, you injure the roots and slow up growth. Shallow cultivation is the rule for gardens.

9. Don't spare the water

Light sprinkling brings roots up to the surface. That's bad. Thorough soaking pushes down to the roots, and keeps them down where they belong. Soak only when the ground is dry.

10. Don't let the weed crop win

Amateur gardeners often dream about dishes full of luscious fresh vegetables the moment they put their seed in. While they dream the weeds sometimes become the major crop.

11. Don't let the bugs beat you to it

Gardeners must be on the alert from beginning to end for insect armies and the onset of disease. Be ready with spray gun and duster and the proper death-dealing ammunition.

MARCH 1, 1942

12. Don't let anything go to waste

If your garden yields too much for you to eat or store or preserve for yourself, see that someone else gets the leftovers. Tell your local Civilian Defense office about your surpluses.

15

To conclude 'what form will our suburban gardens take in the future'.

Chapter 7

Future Gardens and Gardener's

Firstly

Let's consider for a moment that our world is a garden, a place where we humans have been able to grow the food needed to sustain ourselves since Neolithic times. *"Everything changed when farming developed, so dramatic was this change, it is often referred to as [1] "Neolithic agricultural revolution"(James H.S.McGregor 2015 Back to the Garden[1:1]).*

To begin the Neolithic agricultural revolution was when humans changed from hunting and foraging gradually learning to become gardeners and plant wild seed, in confined and protected spaces we call a garden, using first nature principals (*James H.S.McGregor 2015 [1]*).This process happened over hundreds of years, and changed the world forever. Eventually the seed gene was altered through continual sowing and reaping, which allowed early humans to settle and maintain their gardens around their settlements. It was this process which enabled them to grow crops, such as barley, wheat, rye, that have become the mainstay of food that feeds the modern world.

Climate Change and its effect on modern day gardeners (21st century).

The world over climate change is altering the way gardeners and farmers are approaching their profession. In the 20th-21st the agricultural industry world- wide and especially in Australia, is going to have to come to terms with a drier, hotter, and sometimes wetter climate due to melting ice, rising sea levels over extended periods. In 2021 the world is beginning to gain momentum on combating climate change, with forums being organised by the United Nations. The fossil fuel industry and countries with large amounts of emissions are beginning to realise they need to bring their emissions down.

Agricultural and Garden transformation

Over the next few decades, I am in no doubt that suburban and municipal gardens, and the whole of agriculture, will undergo dramatic change; a 'transformation'. I will see in my lifetime (born in 1952). In the 1950's Australia's temperature was 1.95 degrees cooler than Australia's hottest year on record, which was summer 2020. The summer that year temperatures hit 1.52 decrees above average. These fluctuations don't sound much, but what do they mean for the gardeners and agriculturalists of this world?. In the southern hemisphere and in particularly Australia, it will mean a hotter climate and wetter climate. with more severe thunderstorms, more spasmodic heavy rainfall coupled with years of severe droughts.

What will this mean for the future gardener ?

Modern day domestic vegetable gardens will become drier deeper unless organic matter is continually added to reserve soil moisture.

'Water'

Water in Australia and around the world will become a more valuable resource, as it will continue to experience considerable fluctuations in rainfall patterns. Long droughts will be followed by long periods of heavy rainfall patterns particularly on Australia's East Coast. Water storage will be an essential part of a domestic garden or small agricultural property.

In the future it will be crucial for local governments to secure water needed with increasing number of very hot summers. The use of greywater for irrigation might be part of the answer. There will also need be a solution for local sports grounds parks and green space.

The modern allotment / community garden

In the era of high home ownership, developers need to begin leaving space for home owners to grow and form community gardens (the allotment gardens of the early 20th century). This will be where future gardeners can experiment growing their chosen vegetable and flower crops.

I referred in Chapter 5 [ibid]. to Simon Harward's (1572-1614) book "A New Orchard And Garden": The best way for planting, grafting, and to make any ground good, for a rich Orchard.

His book was as crucial for the future of gardening as when he wrote it in the late 1500's, when he reinforced a garden needs to be for flowers, in both Kitchen and Summer gardens. They do not need to have a definite distinction. This attribute is as important today and will be for future gardens as it was in his time.

He says: *Flowers can be intermingled with vegetables such as Onions, Parsnips and all the other vegetables.*

I also commented on [2] L. H. Bailey. Original publication 1923 "Manual of Gardening (Second Edition) / A Practical Guide to the Making of Home Grounds and the Growing of Flowers, Fruits, and Vegetables for Home Use."

This book continues to stand alone for professional gardeners of the future I share a small extract from 1923 referring to a team of horses ploughing a field.

[ibid]*"In places that can be entered with a team of horses deep and heavy ploughing to the depth of seven to ten inches may be desirable. This subsoil plough does not turn a furrow, but a second team draws the implement behind the ordinary plough, with the bottom of the furrow is loosened and broken, the subsoiling and therefore, the subsoil plough should be exceedingly strong. Every pains should be taken to prevent the surface of the land from becoming crusty, for hard surface establish a capillary connection with the moist soil beneath, and is a means of passing off water into the atmosphere"*

The Gardener and his labour

It is the gardener and his labour that needs be acknowledged, with his tools of trade not changing for a millennium. They have been an important part of the history of gardening, hand held hoes, rakes, digging spades and garden forks (all have been refined) have been part of a gardener's toolbox for hundreds of years.

The Gardener's knowledge

In each historical era, we have had to recognise and acknowledge a gardener's knowledge and labour. He or she has been responsible for many innovations and practical elements of horticulture that are taken for granted today. The knowledge needed to prepare soil and make compost for planting and sowing crops, hasn't changed in hundreds of years.

Modern gardeners need skills in designing and maintaining gardens that use less water. They need to learn how to provide for permanent wet boggy areas and 'soak a-ways.'

In the not too distant future providing for a soak a-way will come to the for-front, of garden design.

They need the ability to identify plants, grow trees and shrubs in a home garden, the pruning of trees and shrubs. These qualities all have roots in gardening history, and together they make gardening a valued profession.

Thankfully controlling garden pests and diseases, in an orchard, market garden or garden, has become safer. Not too many years ago, dangerous chemicals for example: lead, and arsenic, were used to control pests, a more organic approach is adhered to today, using a selection of organically based oils.

Garden composting will become an incredibly vital part of vegetable growing in community and private gardens. In many parts of the country is already happening, and is becoming common in many community gardens.

A gardener's compost.

To begin a compost pile, firstly it needs plenty of diverse material(grass clippings, kitchen scrapes, leaves) this bring the earthworms. It needs to be kept damp, this ensures worms and micro -organisms come and bury themselves deep into the active compost. Use a garden fork to regular turn the compost, this quickens the pace of the organic breakdown. With regular turning with a garden fork in 6-8 weeks the material is ready to use in the garden. Adding compost will keep your garden soil organisms active, it will help retain garden moisture. For the future of suburban gardening, it will be vital for gardeners to continue to make their own compost.

Future gardeners and surburban gardens

Gardening will always be one of life's simple pleasures, whether it's growing vegetables flowers, or fruit trees, on a small townhouse patio balcony or surburban garden; or a large community vegetable garden. The outdoor open space will be looking after the local wild life, and nature.

Gardeners and those whom work the land of tomorrow will play a crucial part in the role of establishing humanities future and well-being of our society.

A final word

As in the Neolithic period when early humans hunted and gathered food across their land, to the late middle ages, communities undeniably worked the land with a well- balanced connection to nature.([1]first nature principles:" Back to the Garden James" H.S.Mcgregor.)

It was these early farmers and gardeners who learnt to grow and domesticate wild seed they found among Britain's natural landscapes. This allowed them to settle and into villages and raise food in a garden in-order to survive. They learnt to work and clear the land, with their crude hand tools and an oxen drawn 'primitive' plough.

Gardeners will continue to work the soil and grow produce, connecting them with nature, which is the environment around them. It is a fact in our modern world that early humans had it right in the Neolithic period, with their **'First Nature Principles,** * nourishing themselves and remembering to replenish the earth. These principles are the way to live sustainably on the earth.

[1] *the harmonious interrelationship of human communities and the natural world) first nature principles:" Back to the Garden James H.S.Mcgregor. 2015*

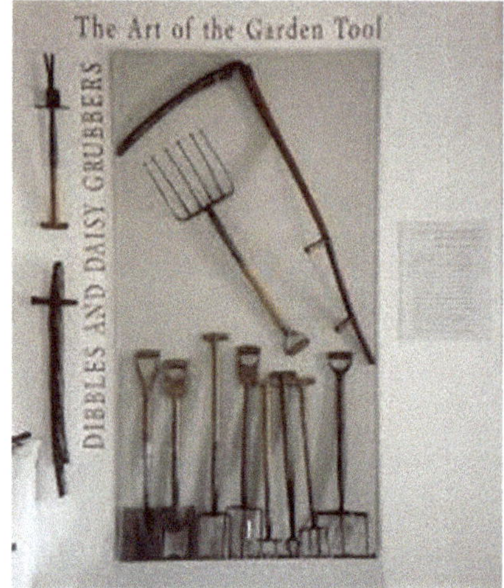

The domestic gardening tool set in the early 19th century.

A 19 century Horse team cutting grass.

The 21 century extra- large tractor team cultivating and seeding a large paddock.

Greenland's ice sheet, beginning to break after the world's modern era warming period.

A modern day formal garden, comprising of circular gardens, with gravel pathways. Iceberg floribunda roses and alyssum feature in the larger circular garden.

Iceberg Roses feature in this small townhouse courtyard garden. Narrow leafed box, (lonicera) make up the feature small hedge.

Tall Hedges make an ideal passage way for the larger garden, notice to a pergola with wisteria is overhead.

Spring at Blenheim Palace garden showing it's upright conifers displaying a feast of Daffodils and Tulips.

A gardener seen here within the formal Rose Garden. With the manicured lawns, these gardens, require a lot of professional care and maintenance.

Hidcote Manor gardens in Gloucestershire Britain is one of the finest gardens owned by the National Trust in Britain. Neatly clipped yew hedging (Taxus)shown here requiring highly skilled gardeners to maintain this garden.

Banks of cold frames, in large gardens ensure trays of early sown flowers and vegetables can be grown on for gardeners to plant out when the frosts are finished.

Rows of outdoor seedling vegetables being planted, using a string line.

On a small market garden Polythene is used to prevent weeds coming through, when planting new seedlings. Polythene tunnels are seen in the distance.

The wind turbine farm, are more are seen now to compete with traditional fossil fuels of the 19th century.

Australia experiencing severe rainfall during summer of 2021 illustrating water flow down a river after heavy rain.

Banks of solar panels illustrate an important energy source for the future.

Lettuce, climbing beans and silverbeet, grown here in a domestic vegetable garden. These vegetable gardens, will continue to be truly valued to feed a family for the foreseeable future.

A domestic compost heap. ensures todays garden has a plentiful supply of organic matter. Each day it needs to be turned by a dedicated gardener.

Strict formality is shown here with this azalea hedge in flower in a suburban garden in 2021 hedge.

Water jets seen here water this large Australian suburban garden.A deciduous conifer features on the lawn.

In modern suburbia here we have a large lawn, featuring a distant view of a country golf course. Large evergreen and deciduous conifers, on the golf course, grow magnificently all through the year. In particularly in a cold climate where they show off their outstanding autumn colour.

Epilogue

My book has now come to a close however, the gardener's journey will continue as long as life continues. Future gardeners will be central to the preservation of our untouched natural environments in both rural and domestic situations. These untouched ecosystems in a city, or town will become central to a future 'well -being' of our society. I wrote regarding about 'second nature', (one's usefulness that become natural to one's self); I also recorded that 'the laws of nature', before human interaction, that was here long before our modern day environmental crisis was upon us. This began sometime during the early 1500's with the advent of the industrial revolution, I stated this was partially caused by the great influx of labour from Britain's countryside to the burgeoning cotton factories of Britain. As the world's cities become ever increasingly larger; tomorrow's societies will live more in high rise apartments or multi- level town houses with little or no open space. In the future open space in towns and cities will become under threat by large property developers. Japan is one country that seems to have the balance right with apartment living combined with open space for the community exercise to ensure their population remains in touch with nature.

To conclude I want to reflect on how integral the gardener has been throughout history. They have been indispensable in the building of social, rural and economic prosperity throughout Britain, and the rest of the world.

In the first three chapters, I focused on the Neolithic civilization, and how they survived in a pristine environment before any human interaction. Over 100's of years the hunter and gatherers had to learn what naturally occurred in nature (for example: seed collection sown and germinating), but not understood by early human's.

Next I concentrated on the middle ages, with the Three Field System. It must be remembered at this time farming, took a giant step forward, with the introduction of a fallow paddock. This was the period I focused on gardener's having a constructive relationships with nature. Monks within their monasteries made a valued contribution to early horticulture and gardening techniques. Their gardeners became a vital source of knowledge throughout whole of the middle ages.

I reflected on the coming of Britain's industrial revolution of the 1600's, that saw the launch of modern agriculture, with the beginning of damaging and destroying pristine environments.

I spoke how allotment vegetable gardens were essential from the beginning of the early 1900's. They made a valued contribution to local societies, during and after the war years. In the future gardeners and small acreage growers I hope will continue to make a significant contribution, to care for earth's landscapes, produce new plants and the maintain of our soils.

Acknowledgments

Almost three years ago this book you see before you arose from an idea of mine, to investigate the beginning of organic gardening. Since then my companion and partner Marilyn has shared a parallel journey of her own in assisting, encouraging and researching my book. The space she allowed me to have at the dining room table, to write the topics of each chapter. Firstly in long hand and then editing /suggesting the many versions of my book's progression. She assisted in choosing pictures that are seen throughout the book and in reaching the ideal caption seen through the time line of history of my book "The Gardener through History"

My sincere thanks.

I searched for a long time for Primary Editor and found 'The write hand man' Keith Maxwood in Canberra A.C.T. he was extremely interested in my topic. His professional editing and writing skills were second to none. I learnt many aspects of effective subject sentence construction through his ability to clearly edit and explain how a chapter or paragraph needs to be constructed. Thankyou

Choosing the pictures throughout book I realised that an Illustrator was also required to enlighten key elements of early British history. Marilyn and I asked Karen Henderson a local artist. Her front and back cover designs are outstanding together with the iron age rock features seen in chapter 1 .My sincere thanks

Finally when the idea of a book came about to give a historical insight of organic gardening a gardening friend Kathe Boehringer was always there to offer advice and encouragement . She gave feedback and manuscript support on the many versions the book went through, finally ending up with this published version. Thank you for your continued interest, support and encouragement, seeing me through to the printed version of "The Gardener through History"

Index

www.ingramcontent.com/pod-product-compliance
Lightning Source LLC
Chambersburg PA
CBHW040535170726
48295CB00012B/482